IVAN

Her Russian Protector, Book One

Roxie Rivera

Night Works Books
College Station, Texas

Night Works Books
3515-B Longmire Drive #103
College Station, Texas 77845
www.roxierivera.com

Publisher's Note: This is a work of fiction. Names, characters, places, and incidents are a product of the author's imagination. Locales and public names are sometimes used for atmospheric purposes. Any resemblance to actual people, living or dead, or to businesses, companies, events, institutions, or locales is completely coincidental.

Book Layout ©2013 BookDesignTemplates.com

Cover Photograph © 2013 Coka/Fotolia.com

Ordering Information:
Quantity sales. Special discounts are available on quantity purchases by corporations, associations, and others. For details, contact the "Special Sales Department" at the address above.

Ivan (Her Russian Protector #1)/ Roxie Rivera. -- 1st ed.
ISBN 978-1-63042-005-5

For David, my sweet Texan protector

1 CHAPTER ONE

"Erin, please don't go in there." Sitting in the front passenger seat, Vivian wrung her hands. "This is way too risky."

My gut clenched at her desperate tone. "I don't have a choice. I have to find Ruby."

"We'll do it some other way." Lena twisted in the driver's seat of her red beater and shot me a pleading look. "Vivi's right. Don't go in there."

I glanced out the rear window of the cramped car. My stomach pitched with anxiety at the sight of the warehouse. Stained with rust, the rundown warehouse sported such a deceptive front. That awful looking place housed one of the finest mixed-martial arts training centers in the world. Men desperate to be champions flew into Houston from all over the world to compete for one of the few open spots every year.

But I wasn't here to join a training regimen. No, I was here because I needed help. The kind of help only a man with his fingers deeply submerged in the murky waters of Houston's seedy underbelly could provide. "I need help."

"These are not the kind of men you go to for help," Vivi insisted. "These are the kind of men you usually need help escaping."

"I'm with Vivi on this one. Don't go looking for trouble, Erin." Lena chewed her thumb. "I mean, Vivi should know. My god, Erin! She works for the Russian mob. She would know what kind of person this Ivan Markovic is."

Vivi thumped Lena's leg. "I don't work for the Russian mob! Jesus, don't say stuff like that. You could get me hurt."

Lena rubbed her leg. "You're a waitress at the Samovar. The place is owned by Nikolai Kalasnikov. If that's not mobbed up, I don't know what is."

"You don't know that for sure," Vivi shot back. "No one really knows if he's in the mob or not. You know how secretive those guys are." Vivi glanced back at me. "When I started working for Nikolai, he warned me to stay away from the men who frequent the restaurant—and I do. Ivan Markovic is a regular customer there. Take Nikolai's advice, Erin. Stay the hell away from Ivan."

IVAN

I appreciated Vivi's warning but it was too late. "I don't have a choice. I'm going in there."

Vivi looked like she was going to burst into tears. Lena sighed loudly. "Keep your phone in your hand and pull up my number. If anything weird happens in there, you hit that button. We'll come in and bust you out."

Any other time I would have laughed at Lena's tough girl remark but, right now, I needed her strength and support. I fished my phone out of my purse and clutched it tightly. "Okay. I'm ready."

Vivi reached back and gripped my wrist. "Whatever you do, don't promise him anything. These Russians are big on honoring their debts. They'll require you to do the same. Remember that he'll expect to collect on whatever you offer."

Armed with Vivi's warning and Lena's promise to save my ass if things went south, I climbed out of the car. A humid May breeze ruffled my skirt. I slid a nervous hand down the front of my dress and finger-combed my short hair. Gulping down the ball of nerves clogging my throat, I pushed my sunglasses into place and forced my feet to move.

The heavy main door proved almost impossible to push open. I threw my willowy frame against it in an attempt to budge the damn thing even an inch. Finally, it slid inward. A blast of frigid air popped me in the face. Entering the warehouse, I couldn't help but wonder if opening that door was the first test for the fighters who made the trek here in their quest for the best trainers.

Once inside the huge space, I lost my courage. The open layout of the gym and sparring cages stunned me. From the outside, this place looked like such a hell hole. Now I understood just how deceptive the dilapidated façade truly was. The interior, though dimly lit, housed expensive equipment. It was teeming with sweaty, half-naked men, some of them working out and others pounding and kicking away at one another in sparring rings.

My appearance didn't go unnoticed. A couple of muscle-heads stopped lifting weights to gawk at me. Feeling self-conscious, I slipped my sunglasses onto the crown of my head and hugged my right arm across my chest. Maybe Vivi was right. This was a bad, bad idea.

"Can I help you?" An older man, old enough to be my grandfather, approached me from one of the nearby workout stations. His heavily accented voice surprised me. It wasn't the mother tongue of Russia that colored his words. No, it was Spanish. "You're lost?"

I shook my head. "I need to see Mr. Markovic."

His white eyebrows arched with surprise. "Ivan? You want to see Ivan?"

I nodded. "Yes, please."

He studied me for a moment before exhaling and flicking his fingers. "Follow me."

I stayed close to the old man as he led me through the warehouse. I kept my gaze glued to the back of his grey t-shirt and refused to meet the curious looks that followed me. Apparently they didn't get a lot of women in this place.

"You wait here." The old man shot me a warning look. "Don't speak."

His instruction made my stomach pitch. Don't speak? What the hell kind of place was this?

Left alone, I dared to lift my gaze to the metal cage before me. It sat on a raised stage and resembled the ones I'd seen on pay-per-view once. Sitting in my then-boyfriend's living room, I hadn't been able to make it through that fight. Seeing it now, being so close I could hear every smack of body contact, left me feeling a bit woozy. Violence and blood had never been things I could easily stomach.

Unlike Vivi and Lena, I'd lived a sheltered life. Until Ruby's recent addiction problems and scrapes with the law, I'd never known anything about the seedy side of Houston. Now I was undergoing a crash course in navigating the very worst the city had to offer.

A shouting man drew my attention. I could hear him clearly even over the music blaring from the sound system. Though I'd never met Ivan Markovic, there was no doubt in my mind that this intimidating man was him.

Standing just outside the cage, he looked so out of place in his perfectly tailored grey trousers and white shirt. The sleeves had been rolled up to his elbows and revealed thickly corded arms emblazoned with tattoos. Even from this distance, the Cyrillic letters were clearly visible. I didn't have to be one of the initiated to understand what they meant.

Ivan clapped his hands and blasted a series of instructions in Russian, the words forceful and demanding. Inside the ring, the fighters didn't dare disobey. They kicked and punched and beat the crap out of one another. As hard as they were going at it, I was glad they were wearing sparring helmets and gloves.

Another man outside the ring whacked together two blocks of wood, signaling the end of the round. Ivan jerked open the cage door and stalked inside. He gestured for the two sweating, panting men to approach him. Hooking his arms around their shoulders, he pulled their heads close together and started to talk to them. I couldn't make out a word he said but the two fighters listened intently.

When he was done with his pointers, Ivan smacked them both on the shoulder and left the cage. He started down the short metal stairs but stopped abruptly. Our gazes clashed. His searing stare burned my skin as it swept me from head to foot. Frowning, he headed down the steps and dipped his head so the old man could speak to him. Not once did his unrelenting gaze leave me.

Trembling inside, I gripped my phone so tightly my fingertips started to go numb. Ivan came so close I could smell the woodsy hints of his cologne. Though not handsome in the most classic sense, Ivan enthralled me. Maybe it was the power and danger that radiated from him. Maybe it was the way he towered over me, those pale blue eyes peering right through me. I don't know—I just couldn't break eye contact with him.

"Look, sweetheart, we've already filled the secretary position." His thickly accented English rolled over me in waves. Because he scared the living daylights out of me, I let the sweetheart pet name slide. Any other guy I would have had no problem correcting but this one? Oh, hell no. He could call me cupcake and I wouldn't even flinch.

"I'm not here for a job, Mr. Markovic."

Surprise filtered across his face. "You want to train?" He laughed, the sound harsh and staccato. "We don't train girls here. Okay? Paco, walk her out."

Desperate, I grasped his wrist and stopped him from walking away from me. The instant we made contact an electric zing arced through me. From the flash in his eyes, he must have felt it, too.

"Please," I begged. "I need your help."

His eyes narrowed. With a swift tug, he freed his wrist from my grasp. With an imperious flick of his fingers, he indicated I should follow him. I scurried to keep up with his long strides. He led me to an office at the rear of the warehouse and gestured for me to enter first. The door closed behind him. He walked to the big window facing out toward the gym and opened the wide horizontal blinds. Apparently he didn't want anyone to get the wrong idea about what was going on in his office.

Certain I was safe with the blinds open, I relaxed a bit. My mouth went dry when he spun to face me. The annoyed expression he wore deflated my hopes.

"Do I know you?" He strode to his desk and leaned back against it. He crossed his muscled arms against his chest and studied me. "I would remember a face like yours. We're not acquainted."

I shook my head. "No, but we have some acquaintances in common. My name is Erin Hanson and my sister, Ruby, is dating one of your trainers. He used to be a fighter but he got all banged up in that car accident last year."

"Andrei?" He looked taken aback. "*Your* sister is the junkie girlfriend?"

I winced at the awful word *junkie*. Sure, Ruby was a pill addict and, yes, she was constantly in trouble trying to support her nasty habit—but I hated to think of her as a junkie. I refused to believe she couldn't be saved or helped. "Yes, my sister is his girlfriend. And, to be fair, Andrei is just as dirty."

Ivan exhaled roughly. His voice was softer, sadder, as he spoke. "Yes. After the car crash, he couldn't fight. I think it was the depression of losing himself that sent him into a pill bottle."

"It was the death of our parents that sent Ruby over the edge. Carbon monoxide," I explained quietly. "I was away at a sleepover but she was supposed to come home that night and probably would have realized something was wrong with Mom and Dad. She didn't come in until after sunrise. By then..."

"I see. You know that Andrei hasn't been in the gym for a week. Maybe longer," Ivan said.

"I know. Ruby has been missing the same amount of time. I went looking for her at Andrei's place but it had been ransacked. So I started hitting up some of the places where I know Ruby likes to score and—"

He held up his hand. "You went to see drug dealers? A nice girl like you?" He shook his head. "This is dangerous. You could get hurt."

I bristled at his insinuation that I was some helpless child. "This isn't the first time I've had to sniff around Houston's back alleys to find my sister. I'm sure it won't be the last. I know what I'm doing."

He shot me a dubious look. "Then why are you here asking me for help?"

"Because I think Ruby and Andrei are in trouble. Big trouble," I emphasized. "Andrei was taking side jobs protecting and driving cargo shipments around town. Stolen cargo," I clarified. "Something went wrong and he screwed up a delivery or stole it." I squeezed my phone even tighter as the murky details raced through my mind. "I've gotten conflicting stories. Either way, Ruby was with him. Now they're both missing—and I think they're in trouble."

Ivan's jaw visibly tightened and released. "Who was Andrei running cargo for?"

"I don't know. I've heard three different versions and none of them are good." I nervously chewed my bottom lip and decided to lay it all on the line. "It may have been the Albanians."

Not even a man as tough as Ivan could hide the shock of that tidbit. The corners of his mouth tightened. "You're sure?"

"Not absolutely but I think it's true. Why else would people literally run from me when I start asking questions about Andrei and Ruby?"

"So why come to me, Erin?"

"I need someone to help me get information. No one will talk to me anymore. They're afraid."

"For good reason," he interjected. "Do you have any idea what kind of people you're dealing with, Erin?"

My heart stammered in my chest. "Yes, I do."

"Then I don't know why you're here. You think I'm going to get involved with the Albanian mob over a couple of thieving junkies?" He pointed to a sign prominently displayed on his office wall that proclaimed the space clean. "I run a clean gym, okay? No drugs. No steroids. Andrei and your sister brought that poison into my gym. I lost three fighters this week for failing drug tests. *Three*! That's my ass on the line, my reputation." He shook his head. "I left that life behind. I'm not going back."

The last glimmer of hope faded within me. Feeling stupid for even thinking this man might help me, I offered a timid, apologetic smile. "I'm sorry, Mr. Markovic. I shouldn't have—well. Thank you for your time."

Facing burning with embarrassment, I headed for the door. I couldn't get out of there fast enough. What the hell had I been thinking? Was I really expecting a man like Ivan to put his neck on the line to help a stranger?

"Erin." He spoke my name in that low, rumbling voice. "Come back."

I swallowed hard before pivoting on my heel to face him. He stood in the doorway of his office. The resigned look on his face didn't exactly inspire confidence. Still, if he was reconsidering, I had to try to convince him.

I slipped by him and back into the room. His scent, that masculine mix of cologne and sweat, enveloped me. I became intensely aware of his body heat and his hulking frame. I was close enough now I could see all the faded scars along his jaw and neck. Lower down, I saw the smallest hint of a tattoo peeking out from the neckline of his shirt.

He closed the door again and put a hand on it. The tattoos on his fingers and wrist looked so stark against his paler skin. His gaze bore into me. I tried not to squirm with discomfort. Finally, he sighed loudly. "Look, I'll ask around, okay? I can't make you any promises."

Overcome with relief, I felt the burning prickle of tears stinging my eyes. "Thank you, Mr. Markovic." I blinked quickly as the wetness spilled onto my cheeks. "I'm just grateful that you're willing to help me."

"Ivan," he corrected. He hesitated before wiping away the slick tears dripping down my face. His rough thumb rasped my skin, his very touch branding me. "You should call me Ivan."

IVAN

I held my breath as his thumb wiped away the last remnants of my relieved tears. He seemed impossibly tall and so primal and male as he loomed over me. I gazed up into his harsh face and saw the briefest glimmer of something in his light eyes. I couldn't place it. Sadness? Longing?

He pulled away suddenly and stalked to his desk. He returned with a notepad and pen. "Write down your number and address."

"Okay." I neatly printed my information on the yellow paper and handed it back to him.

"You will go home and you will wait."

"For what?"

"For my call," he explained. "You will not involve yourself in this matter again. Understood?"

"But she's my sister and I—"

"No." He interrupted me with a slash of his hand through the air. "These are the terms I require."

I sensed he wasn't a man used to being defied. "All right. I'll go home and wait."

"Good."

Something he said made me curious. Vivi's warning echoed in my head. *He'll expect to collect.* "Ivan, what other terms do you require?"

His gaze snapped to my face. Eyes narrowed, he asked, "What do you mean?"

17

Awash in anxiety, I clarified, "Are you going to want to be paid for your services?"

He looked annoyed. "Let's find your sister first. We'll worry about compensation later."

I wanted to press him for specifics but he ushered me to the door. Uncertainty settled into the pit of my stomach. What would he want when this was all over and Ruby was safe? Better yet, would I be willing or able to give it to him?

Silently, Ivan walked me to the middle of the gym. I took the hint and quickly scurried toward the exit. Every gaze in the place seemed glued to me. I kept my gaze fixed forward and put one foot in front of the other, my caramel-colored ballet flats moving whisper-soft against the gleaming wood floor.

This time I managed to open the door without too much of a fight. I cast one final glance over my shoulder and met Ivan's piercing gaze. I slipped my sunglasses back into place and left the building.

But as I walked to Lena's car, I couldn't shake the feeling I'd just made a deal with the devil.

IVAN

Ivan watched Erin as she hurried to the exit. He didn't blame her for moving so quickly. That she'd been brave enough to come into his gym and ask for his help still shocked him. There weren't many people who would do something so brazen.

Try as he might, Ivan couldn't stop his gaze from dropping to the enticing swing of her hips. The pale blue skirt of her dress swished against her thighs. Those shapely legs and her tight ass were hard to ignore. Innocent as she looked, Ivan had no doubt that Erin was going to be big trouble.

"Kostya." He gestured for the wiry, dark-haired man to come close for his instruction. "Follow the girl. Keep her out of trouble."

Nodding, Kostya left to trail Erin. Ivan caught Dimitri's gaze. They'd been friends long enough to communicate silently. Ivan didn't even check to make sure Dimitri followed him back to the office. The certainty that Dimitri would be there was absolute.

Dimitri shut the door behind him. In rapid-fire Russian, he asked, "What did she want? Who the hell is she?"

"You know the girl Andrei dates?"

"The junkie?'

Ivan remembered the pain that flashed across Erin's face when he'd used the word. It was the first time in a long time that he'd experienced any guilt, however fleeting. "Yes. That's her sister, Erin. Ruby is missing and so is Andrei."

'They're probably passed out in a crack house."

"Possibly," Ivan agreed. "Erin asked for my help in finding them. She thinks it's something more sinister."

"And that would be?"

"The Albanians."

"You're not serious." Dimitri looked perturbed. "You told her no?"

"I told her I'd look into it. I made no promises."

Dimitri cursed in frustration. "What happened to your number one rule? Huh? Don't get involved, right?"

Ivan asked himself the same thing. There was something about Erin. He couldn't put his finger on it and couldn't explain it. Wiping the tears from her face had left his heart racing and his lower belly clenching. Was it her soft, green eyes imploring him to help that melted through the icy shield he'd erected around himself? Was it her pink pout and the thoughts of claiming her full mouth? Was it that bright citrus scent of her perfume that wound around him and invaded his senses? He didn't know. He only knew that he felt a connection to her, one that couldn't be denied.

"I'm making an exception." Ivan shot Dimitri a look that warned him to let this one go and not point out his hypocrisy. "Get out on the street and find Andrei and this girl, Ruby. Okay?"

"Yeah. Fine." Dimitri sounded pissed but he would do as told. "And you?"

Ivan rolled down his sleeves so he could slip into his jacket. "I'm going to the Samovar. I have to see Nikolai."

2 CHAPTER TWO

A few hours later, I climbed out of my car and bumped the door closed with my hip. I glanced around the parking lot of the grocery store and hit the lock button on my key fob. Since leaving the gym, I couldn't shake the feeling that I was being followed. I'd said the same thing to Lena when she'd dropped me off at my apartment and she'd looked at me like I was a total loon—but I don't know. Something didn't feel right.

Even after scanning the well-lit parking lot of the supermarket twice, I didn't see anything. Maybe Lena was right. Maybe I was losing it.

Though I still couldn't stop thinking about Ruby, I had to keep living. That meant working and eating. I had the weekend off thankfully but my fridge was totally empty and the pantry shelves were just as bare. The urge to stuff my cart with junk food overwhelmed me. Maybe I could obliterate my fears and worries with a super-sized dose of hydrogenated oils and carbohydrates.

I grabbed a cart and pushed it down the first produce aisle. My purse started to sing and vibrate wildly. Recognizing the muffled ring tone as the one I'd assigned to Vivi, I stopped and dug around in my purse in search of my phone. "Hello?"

"Hey! It's me."

I smiled and rifled through my bag for the short shopping list I'd jotted down before leaving my apartment. "I know. What do you need?"

"Just thought you'd like to know that Ivan was here earlier."

"Here? Where? The Samovar?"

"Yeah."

"And?"

"He met with Nikolai at the corner table," Vivi said, her voice soft and conspiratorial. No doubt she was hiding in a linen closet or bathroom stall at the restaurant to make her secret phone call. "I couldn't hear everything. They only wanted tea so I came to the table twice and that was it. I heard your name a few times and Andrei's." She paused. "Nikolai wasn't happy and Ivan left pretty pissed off, Erin."

My stomach flip-flopped. "You're sure?"

"Oh yeah. It's that look they get in their eyes. Cold, you know? Just be careful, Erin."

"I will."

"Why don't you come stay with me and Lena tonight? We'll feel better if you're safe at our place."

"I'm fine, Vivi. Stop worrying. You're going to give yourself an ulcer." I pushed my cart forward. "I'm buying groceries and heading home. That's it."

"Text me when you're safe inside your apartment, okay?"

I rolled my eyes. "Yeah. Okay. I'll talk to you later."

"Bye."

"Bye." I dropped my phone back into my purse and finished my shopping. The store wasn't very busy but there were only a handful of checkout lanes open. I ended up four carts back and smack dab in the middle of the magazine aisle. A home decorating magazine caught my eye. I flipped through the pages of gorgeous interiors and lusted after the beautiful homes. The small two room apartment I shared with Ruby would fit in most of the sumptuously photographed kitchens.

My cell phone started rattling around in my purse again. Certain it was Vivi calling to see why I hadn't texted her yet, I jabbed my hand in my bag and swiped my finger across the screen while bringing it to my ear. "Look, Vivi, I'm still in line—"

"Erin!"

My eyes widened at the sound of Ruby's voice. "Ruby! Where are you?"

"Oh god. I'm in so much trouble."

"Just tell me where you are." I pushed my cart out of line and left it near the end-cap of lighters and charcoal. I flashed one of the employees an apologetic smile and mouthed *I'm sorry* before rushing out of the grocery store.

"I don't know. It's, um, it's a house. Andrei brought me here to hide out but he left this morning and never came back."

My stomach lurched. Was Andrei dead? "Can you get to a window? Can you see anything outside? Maybe a restaurant or a building or a store or something?"

"It's a street. Like a subdivision, I think." She sounded groggy and was probably coming down from a nasty high. "The house across the street is brick. The number is 16114."

I tried not to get aggravated with her but it was hard to keep cool. "Can you see a street sign?"

"Um..."

I climbed into my car, locked the door and stabbed the key into the ignition. "Ruby?"

"Harmony Fields."

I scrunched up my face. "What? Is that the street name?"

"There's a sign on the corner. It's limestone and wood."

"The subdivision name?" I put her on speaker and Googled the name of the subdivision. The address was clear across town. "Okay. I know where you are."

"My battery is dying."

I cursed softly as I backed out of my parking spot. "Okay. Why don't you go ahead and hang up to save battery. I'll be there in fifteen minutes, maybe twenty. Just stay put."

"What if Andrei comes back?"

Even though I wanted to punch that rat bastard in the balls for dragging Ruby into his organized crime mess, I knew she wouldn't come with me unless I protected him, too. "I'll bring him back to our apartment. You'll both be safe there."

"Promise?" She sounded so childlike and nothing like the big sister I'd once known her to be.

"I promise, Ruby."

IVAN

"Okay. I'll see you soon."

"Yes. Bye. Be careful." I dropped my phone into the cup holder and left the parking lot. My stomach knotted painfully as I navigated the early evening traffic. On a hot, humid Friday like this the clubs and restaurants would be packed. Vehicles jammed the roadways. I had to cross some of the busiest intersections to reach Ruby. My gaze darted from my dashboard clock to the windshield and back again. I prayed she'd be safe just a little while longer.

But what the hell was she doing in that part of town? It was a middle-class neighborhood and definitely not one where I would have ever looked for her. Ruby might not have been abusing hard drugs like meth or heroin or cocaine but the places where she and her pill-popping, pill-snorting friends hung out and scored weren't very nice. They definitely weren't two and three hundred thousand dollar houses...

My gaze flitted briefly to my rearview mirror. A black SUV followed me through a left turn. Paranoia gripped me. Hadn't I seen that SUV in the parking lot of the supermarket? I tried to convince myself that I was crazy. I mean, there were a lot of SUVs in Texas, right? But something wasn't right about this one.

As if confirming my worst fears, the SUV turned into the Harmony Fields subdivision and crawled along behind me as I searched for the right house. Did I dare park and run inside to find Ruby? What if this was one of the bad guys? Had I just led them right to her?

Instead of stopping, I kept right on driving and picked up my cell phone. I dialed Ruby as I drove along the street to the end of the cul-de-sac. Spotting a for sale sign, I parked in front of the vacant house and pretended to be looking at the property. Why wasn't Ruby answering?

I glanced in my rearview mirror. The black SUV drove slowly by me but I didn't dare make eye contact through my window. I kept my gaze fixed on the house and pretended to be studying it intently. The SUV made the turn of the cul-de-sac and turned off a side street. I waited another few minutes before putting my car in drive again and heading back to the house where Ruby hid.

I found 16114 and parked across the street at 16115, the house where Ruby must have been. It was a small brick ranch house that looked innocuous enough. I twisted in my seat to check the street. Everything was quiet.

Phone in hand and ready to dial 9-1-1 at the first hint of trouble, I exited my car and locked the doors behind me. Keys in hand, I suddenly wished I'd done what most of my friends had done on their twenty-first birthdays and treated myself to a concealed handgun class and a small pistol for my purse. A year ago, I'd never dreamed I'd find myself in a situation like this. Now I was silently cursing myself for not being more proactive. What if Ruby wasn't alone in there?

My finger hesitated just above the doorbell. Should I? Uncertain, I tried the door knob and found it unlocked. Gathering my courage, I pushed the door open. "Ruby?"

There was no answer so I stepped inside the house. Almost instantly, the overpowering scent of chemicals took my breath away. *What the hell?*

"Ruby! Where are you? Hurry up! Let's go."

The fine hairs on the back of my neck stood on end as I slowly crept across the living room. One glance into the kitchen and I had my answer to the strange smell question. The counters and table top were littered with empty bottles and boxes and equipment. Someone had been cooking meth in here. Small batches, it seemed, but just as dangerous.

I shoved down the urge to throttle Ruby for pulling me into this nightmare. I wasn't sure how volatile the remnants of the drug-making procedure were but I didn't dare turn on any lights as I continued my snail's pace walk toward the rear bedrooms. There was still enough light from the setting sun to illuminate the interior of the house but I walked carefully.

Worried she'd passed out or gotten high again, I had to check every room and closet and even under the beds. When she was high, Ruby often squeezed herself into tight spaces. I didn't understand it and probably never would.

I came to the last bedroom in the house and spotted the hot pink phone she carried everywhere. The sight of used syringes, spoons and crushed pills left me cold. Ruby's preferred method of abusing oxy had always been snorting, especially the quick-release form of the drug. Now it seemed she'd made the jump to shooting up the pills.

I picked up the empty bottle and used the last rays of sunshine streaming through the open blinds to check the label. The name I recognized as one of the aliases she sometimes used when doctor shopping.

A few months earlier, she'd somehow managed to buy an MRI and took it to pain clinics around town for prescriptions. Even though I'd gone through her things dozens of times, I'd never been able to find the damn MRI. Not that it would have done any good. She would have bought another one or simply scored her pills from some lowlife street dealer.

The prescription had been filled the day before and was already empty. Ninety pills gone. Had Ruby taken them all in forty-eight hours? Had she shared some with Andrei? Gut clenching so hard I couldn't breathe, I bravely pushed open the door of the bathroom, fully expecting to find Ruby passed out on the cold tile—or worse.

But the bathroom was empty. I shoved aside the shower curtain and discovered only a filthy tub, the tile and grout so stained with mildew they were an unsightly greenish-black. I let the curtain fall and left the bathroom. Where the hell had Ruby gone?

The second I stepped back into the bedroom I spotted him. A strange man, short and stocky, stood in the doorway of the bedroom. He held a very long, very sharp knife. Heart beating in my throat, I croaked, "Who are you?"

"I should ask you same question." His accent sounded so different than the Russian I'd heard earlier today. Was it Albanian? I couldn't tell. "What you do here?"

His broken English came through loud and clear. "I'm looking for my sister."

He chuckled menacingly and took cautious strides my way. "Red-haired slut, yes?"

I gulped in fear and backed into the corner. Ruby had recently dyed her normally straw-blonde hair a vibrant shade of red but she most definitely was not a slut. "Her name is Ruby and she's missing."

"Not missing," he said, his vicious smile almost stopping my heart. "Just misplaced."

"Misplaced? What does that—?"

Heavy footsteps in the hallway interrupted us. In a flash of grey fabric, Ivan appeared in the doorway behind the man. He took one look at me and flew at the knife-wielding man. With the skill and practice of a man used to the hard life of the streets, Ivan expertly rid the shorter man of his weapon and tossed him into the wall. He popped the man twice in the temple and once in the nose, leaving him dazed and bloodied. The brutal strength Ivan displayed shocked me.

As the man grunted and tried to climb to his feet another man ran into the room behind Ivan. I recognized the thin, dark-haired man from the gym. He spoke quickly to Ivan in Russian. Whatever he'd said, it wasn't good.

Ivan grabbed my hand and pulled me behind him. His hand moved to my hip, the gesture simultaneously possessive and protecting. The sound of footsteps echoed in my ears. More men spilled into the bedroom. Hidden behind Ivan, I silently prayed that we'd make it out of here alive.

"Ivan."

"Besian." His fingers bit into the flesh of my hips. I didn't dare move. The man had just put his body between mine and danger. I wasn't going to do anything to risk his. "We were leaving."

"I have business with the girl."

"Not this one."

IVAN

The man, Besian, laughed. "You're the second person today to tell me to keep away from her. What's so special about this one, huh?"

"She belongs to me." His words, spoken so cold and calm, shocked me. *Belonged to him?*

"I see." Besian sounded surprised. That made two of us. "I have to ask her questions, Ivan."

"Then you go through me." His voice remained steady as he delivered his threat. I wasn't sure how much weight it carried but apparently it was enough.

"Hey, Ivan," Besian said with a nervous laugh, "we're old friends, yeah?" Ivan said nothing. "Look, we don't have to escalate this, okay? Just ask her how she knew her sister was here."

"Erin, how did you know your sister was here?" Ivan's tone warned me not to lie.

Voice trembling, I answered them. "She called. She said Andrei had abandoned her. She wasn't here when I arrived."

"There. Satisfied, Besian?"

"For now," the other man said. "You understand that Andrei and the sister are in blood with us now. If that debt isn't settled..."

The man's threat hung in the air. The chilling words spilled over me and left me shaking. I didn't know what *in blood* meant but I figured it was bad. Really bad.

Ivan didn't say anything. He simply grasped my hand and tugged me along behind him. His friend, the dark-haired man who had come running in to warn us, flanked me. The men kept me surrounded and safe as we left the house. I spotted four black SUVs parked outside and my small silver car in the center. One of the SUVs had two men waiting in it. Ivan flicked his fingers and the man in the passenger seat quickly came to the sidewalk.

Ivan spun around and stuck out his hand. "Keys. Now."

I could hear the anger in his voice and didn't dare tell him no. I slapped my keys into his palm. He tossed them to the man he'd summoned from the waiting SUV and gave him instructions. Still holding my hand, Ivan led me to the other SUV and opened the rear passenger door. He picked me up like a small child and dropped me in the seat. "Seatbelt."

With shaking hands, I buckled up. The dark-haired man climbed into the driver's seat and Ivan hopped onto the passenger seat to my right. His annoyed expression didn't bode well.

Vivi and Lena's warnings circled round and round in my head. There was no escaping the consequences this time. I was in big fucking trouble.

IVAN

Ivan tried to muscle down his anger and fought the urge to shout at Erin for being so reckless. She'd just survived a shocking experience and still hadn't located her sister. It was clear she was in a delicate state. The last thing he wanted to do was scare her even more— and he never wanted her to be afraid of him. His size and brute strength had always frightened people, women especially. Somehow the thought of Erin flinching away from him seemed even more agonizing.

It was stupid, really, his attraction to her. This petite pixie with her short, dark hair and bright green eyes wasn't the kind of woman for a man like him. Nikolai had known of her when they'd had their sit down earlier. She was close friends with the black-haired waitress Nikolai all but considered his ward. If Erin hung out with Vivian, that meant she was intelligent and probably well-educated. In other words, she was much too good for him.

He tried not to examine his reasons for wanting to protect Erin. It wasn't just that she was innocent and sweet and soft and the perfect prey for a man like Besian and his thugs. No, it was something even more dangerous than that. He'd already let his attraction to her put him in an impossible position.

"I'm sorry, Ivan."

Her faint, warbling voice cut him deeply. Was she crying because she was afraid of him? Was she crying because she feared she'd never see her sister again or because the strained meeting with Besian had shaken her? He didn't ask because he wasn't sure he'd like the answer.

Still he had to know why she'd done something so incredibly stupid. "What were you thinking coming here? Didn't I tell you to stay home and let me deal with this?"

The lights from the dashboard and the street lamps illuminated her face. She bravely met his questioning gaze. "I was shopping when Ruby called me. She was scared and alone. I wasn't going to waste time trying to find you." Her shoulders sagged and her head dropped. "But that doesn't matter because I was too late."

The urge to comfort her gripped him. He wanted nothing more than to pull her onto his lap and kiss away the pain tearing at her—but he didn't. She needed to know how serious the situation had become.

"Do you know who those men were?"

She shook her head. "No."

"Besian and his crew enforce for the Albanian mob. They're some of the most dangerous men you'll ever meet." He didn't mention that she was riding in a vehicle with two men more dangerous than Besian because she wouldn't understand. "You are lucky that I had Kostya following you and he was able to call me. I was only a few minutes away otherwise..."

"I knew it!" She shouted triumphantly and turned her attention to the driver seat. "I knew someone was following me."

"You had the sense to know you were being tailed but didn't have the sense to know that you shouldn't go into a strange house alone?" Ivan marveled at the poor choice she'd made. "I know you love your sister but you'll be no use to her dead."

"I said I was sorry. What more do you want from me?"

That was the question of the night, wasn't it?

"I want you to be safe. I want you to be *smart*. Look, you heard Besian. Your sister is in blood—"

"What does that mean?"

He frowned at her interruption. "The Albanians live by an honor code. Your sister stole from them. She also got two of their men killed. She's a walking target. If they don't find her and Andrei..."

"They'll come for me." She finished his thought with a shaky voice. "I didn't know about her killing anyone."

"Then I guess you didn't know that Ruby and Andrei were using the money they skimmed from the stolen cargo deliveries to start their own criminal enterprise."

Erin reeled back as if she'd been slapped. "*What?*"

"Yes," he said unhappily. "Ruby and Andrei were using the money to buy product that they sold on the street."

"Product?"

"Pills. Cocaine. Meth. They undercut the price of the dealers in the area they targeted and were making money hand over fist. But they made one big mistake."

"What was that?" Fear colored her voice.

"They were dealing in Hermanos territory." Ivan knew the Latin street gang by reputation. They weren't people to be fucked with and Ruby and Andrei had been taunting them for weeks now. "The Hermanos assumed the Albanians were trying to move in on their business and shot up one an Albanian captain's house. That's why Ruby and Andrei ran. They've got the Albanians and the Hermanos coming for them now."

"You're sure?" Ivan shot her a look. "Of course you're sure," she whispered. A second later, she leaned

forward and tapped Kostya's arm. "You should probably pull over and let me out now."

"What?" Ivan carefully grasped her upper arm and
forced her to meet his gaze. "What makes you think
I'm going to let you out on the street, Erin?"

"You said I'm as good as dead. I can't put anyone
else at risk, Ivan." Her eyes glistened with tears. "Look,
you don't even know me. I'm just some stupid girl
with a drug addict sister, right? You don't owe me any
favors. Just let me out and give me my car back. I'll
figure this out on my own."

"The hell you will," he snapped. The sincerity in
her eyes chilled him. She was ready to go out there
and face two vicious gangs on her own rather than put
another life in the crosshairs. He couldn't allow it. He
wouldn't allow it. "I told you I'd find your sister."

"You didn't make me any promises, Ivan. Remember?"

Oh, he remembered all right. That was before Erin
had wormed her way inside his mind. Visions of her
beautiful face had haunted him all afternoon. Finding
her facing off with that bastard in the meth house had
sent him into a rage. No one was ever going to harm
her. Of that, he was absolutely certain.

"The terms of our agreement have changed." He
made his decision unilaterally. "You're coming home

with me. I'm going to keep you safe until this thing with your sister reaches a satisfactory end."

"But—"

He lifted his hand. "No. You don't know anything about this world you've stumbled into but I'm all too familiar with it. You're coming with me and that's that."

Her lips parted on a protest but she didn't fight him. She was smart enough to know that she needed him. He wondered what would happen when she was safe again. Would she walk out of his life as easily and quickly as she'd barged into it?

"Did you mean it?" She asked some time later, her voice gentle and uncertain.

He glanced at her shadowed face, the dashboard lights and street lamps barely illuminating her now. "Mean what?"

She hesitated. "That I belong to you."

He didn't even have to glance at the rearview mirror to know Kostya was watching them with interest. He ignored the driver and focused only on her. He didn't know what she wanted to hear or even what he was comfortable confirming or denying. This whole thing was one complicated mess and he was still searching for sure footing with her.

Finally, he managed an answer. "For now."

3 CHAPTER THREE

An hour later, I wiped my hand across the foggy mirror and stared at my reflection. Standing naked and
wet in one of Ivan's guest bathrooms, I felt incredibly
off-kilter. I don't think I ever could have imagined my
night would end like this. How the hell had this night
gone so wrong? I'd been *this close* to finding Ruby but
she'd vanished without a trace.

Maybe that was a good thing. She'd obviously
evaded the Albanians who were hot on her tail. If
she'd been there when I'd arrived, they would have
grabbed us both or separated us or worse—possibly

even killed us right there. Maybe she could stay safe a little longer. I didn't doubt Ivan would find her. He didn't strike me as the kind of man to break a promise.

I couldn't shake the feeling that something was happening between us. Something *real*. I'd never had such an instant connection to any man. He definitely wasn't the sort I normally crushed on or dated. Ivan was…well…he was complicated, wasn't he?

It was obvious that the rumors about him were true. He was a man who had once been deeply involved in Houston's criminal underworld. He'd probably been involved in it way back in Russia, too. Those tattoos weren't just for show. The way the Albanians—that man, Besian, especially—had caved to him hadn't escaped me. Ivan said Besian was one of the most dangerous men I'd ever meet. What did that say about Ivan?

I'd noticed the way he'd purposely kept his voice low and even with me during the car ride to his house. Even though anger had been radiating off him in waves, he hadn't once lost control. I sensed he was a man who was always in complete control of himself. In a way, it was infuriating. He wasn't giving me any reasons to dislike him or distance myself. If anything, I found him even more intriguing.

IVAN

The sound of my phone ringing pulled me out of the guest bathroom. Towel wrapped tightly around my body, I headed into the attached bedroom and found my phone on the bed next to my purse. Vivi's face filled my phone's screen.

"Hello?'

"Oh my god! Are you okay? What happened? Should we come over?"

"Vivi, calm down! I'm okay."

"Are you sure? I was getting off shift and Nikolai wouldn't let me take the bus home. He had his driver bring me to the apartment. I asked why and he told me what happened." Vivi sounded close to tears. "Are you sure you're okay?"

"I'm fine." I sat down on the bed and slumped forward with a loud sigh. "Ruby called me. I was so close but I missed her. By minutes, I'm guessing. And then that man showed up and Ivan got there in time to save me. It was scary but Ivan kept me safe. He protected me."

"I could just smack you, Erin! We told you to call us if you needed help. I mean, come on! At least Lena packs heat."

"I know." I cringed at my stupidity. "But I was so worried Ruby would run or pass out or something. You know how she is."

"Yeah," Vivi said, her voice unnaturally soft. "When this is over, when she's safe and everything is okay again, you're going to have to make some hard choices about her. You can't keep enabling her."

Any other time, I would have argued with Vivi but not tonight. She was right. "I keep thinking about how crazy this has all become. I always want to save her. I'm always running around cleaning up after Ruby. I should have...I should have cut her loose a long time ago, I think."

The pained sob that escaped my throat was filled with years of grief and anguish. How many times had Ruby stolen from me? How many times had I come home to find her druggie friends passed out on our couch? How many times had her dealers accosted me or shaken me down for her owed debts? This thing now was just a culmination of years of bad choices—bad choices I'd supported by enabling her with a place to stay and money.

"She's your sister, Erin." Vivi sniffled on the other end of the phone, no doubt crying right along with me. Unlike Lena who held everything inside and refused to show any emotion, Vivi showed such warmth and empathy for people. "We do stupid things for the people we love."

I thought about the drug-addled, mentally ill mother who had nearly killed Vivi as a child and the father who had chosen his life with a hardcore outlaw motorcycle gang over her. The same father who had manipulated a twelve-year-old Vivi into helping him run drugs. To be betrayed and used in that way was a stain that never washed off. If anyone understood what I was going through right now, it was Vivi.

"I've tried to get her help so many times. I've dragged her to meetings. I've taken her to doctors for help detoxing at home. Remember when I worked three jobs last summer to pay for ninety days of rehab? She didn't even last a full month."

"Maybe this will be the nightmare that pushes her to change. Hopefully she'll finally wake the fuck up and see how badly these drugs are ruining her life and yours."

I wasn't so sure. I'd assumed a nasty overdose last summer and a brush with drug court earlier in the year would have done it but neither had touched her.

"So where are you now?"

"I'm at Ivan's house."

"Oh. Wow."

"Yeah."

"So I guess you're really safe, huh?"

"Seems that way."

"Well—what's his house like? I mean, you know, like is it obnoxiously huge with all the money he's made with his gym and his fighters?"

"It's big," I confirmed. "It's very beautifully furnished and very nice."

"And Ivan?"

"He's been very nice to me. He didn't have to put his neck on the line with those Albanians but he did."

There was a pause on the other end of the line. Finally, Vivi asked, "Do you think he like, you know, *likes* you?"

I swallowed hard. "Yes."

"And you? Do you like him?"

"Yes. No?" I rubbed my forehead. "Maybe?"

Vivi laughed. "Well which one is it, Erin?"

"Yes," I said finally. "I do. Don't get me wrong. He's big and scary but there's just something about him. It's in his eyes. He's...vulnerable."

"Vulnerable? Ivan Markovic?" Vivi practically guffawed. "You've never seen that guy fight. I hear he's a vicious beast, Erin."

"I don't doubt it but I'm not talking about his skills with his fists. I'm talking about emotionally. I think he's vulnerable that way."

"Aren't we all?"

Vivi had me there. "Yeah, I guess."

"You know I'm right. Look, I've got to go. I've got laundry to finish and I'm going in to work the morning shift tomorrow."

"Why so many hours this week?"

"Supplies," Vivi said. "I'm working on something new and beautiful but it's different and bigger. I need more canvas and paints. It all adds up."

"Something for a new show maybe?"

"Maybe," she said coyly. "You'll have to wait and see."

"Tease!"

"Ha! But, speaking of teasing, be careful with Ivan. If he's interested in you and you're interested in him, it could get complicated, Erin. He's not the only one that's vulnerable right now."

As always, she gave wise advice far above her twenty-one years. "Duly noted, Vivi."

We said our goodbyes. I headed back into the bathroom and slipped into the grey t-shirt and black boxers Ivan had lent me. One of his men was supposed to bring me some things from my apartment but he hadn't returned yet. Ivan's boxers were huge on me so I fished around in my purse for a couple of silver snap hair clips and used them to gather and pinch the extra fabric on one side of my waist.

Satisfied with my borrowed clothing, I left the bedroom in search of Ivan. He'd fixed me a sandwich earlier in the kitchen and had given me a quick tour of the place on the way up to the guest room. In the hallway off the living room, Kostya spotted me. Without a word, he pointed to a room at the end of the corridor. I nodded and smiled, silently thanking him for his help.

I rapped my knuckles against the paneled door and waited. Ivan said something in Russian I didn't understand. His tone sounded inviting enough so I twisted the knob and pushed the door open. I found Ivan sitting behind a desk. The bright white glow of two computer monitors sitting on the far right side of his desk painted him with light. He seemed irritated with something. I just hoped it wasn't me.

He didn't look up until after I'd closed the door behind me. His eyes widened slightly when he caught sight of me leaning against the door. "Erin."

"Hey." I gestured to the door. "I can go if you're busy."

He shook his head. "No, I'm just working out some training issues at the gym. Losing three fighters opened up some spots. Now I have fighters asking to be shuffled around to different trainers and others trying to get into the gym."

"I see."

His interested gaze roamed me. The corners of his mouth lifted in a smile. "You look better in those clothes than I ever have."

I laughed nervously and played with the front of the cotton shirt. "Thanks by the way."

He waved his hand. "It's no trouble."

"You know it is," I countered. "I've caused you a lot of trouble in the last, oh, eight hours or so." I hesitated before asking, "Do you regret it?"

"Helping you?" He shook his head. "No."

"Are you sure?"

Ivan studied me a moment. Finally, he flicked his thick fingers. "Come here, Erin."

Mouth dry, I crossed the distance between us. Ivan pointed at the empty spot on his desk. I hopped up onto it and self-consciously tugged the hem of his borrowed shirt down against my thighs. He leaned back in his chair and asked, "What are you going to do after we find your sister?"

I considered his question. "Vivi just asked me the same thing."

His brow furrowed. "Short girl? Black hair? Works at Samovar?"

I nodded. "She knows you."

"She should," he said with a laugh. "I always tip well."

I smiled at him. "I'm sure she appreciates it."

"She better," he joked. "Every time I leave there, my wallet is noticeably lighter."

I was surprised by the way smiling and laughter softened his harsh features. I rather liked this new glimpse into Ivan. Maybe he was all tough and scary on the outside but soft and sweet on the inside.

With a long, slow exhale, I said, "I don't know what I'm going to do after we find Ruby. I'll probably try to talk her into rehab again."

"It won't work." Ivan spoke with such certainty. "*She* has to *want* to change. She has to want to kick the drugs. You can't do it for her."

I picked at the hem of the shirt. "I used to think that if I just loved her more and supported her and showed her that she had so many reasons to get clean she would. Now I'm not so sure."

"Look, I've never been addicted to drugs or alcohol but I know how hard it is to make a change. I know how difficult it is to walk away from a certain kind of life and start a new, different one. It's terrifying."

I lifted my gaze to his. "You mean when you left the mob?"

Ivan's unwavering gaze held mine. "Yes."

"Why?"

"Why did I leave?" He sucked in a noisy breath. "I'd never enjoyed that life. Some men do. It was never one I wanted. It was a necessity."

"Necessity? How?"

"Back in Russia, we grew up in an orphanage. You can't even imagine how awful it was."

I could actually. I'd seen news reports on the current state of some Russian orphanages. I could only imagine what they were like thirty years ago.

"You said we. Who is we?"

"Nikolai and Yuri and Dimitri," he explained. "We were all there together as boys. We ran away as teen-agers. Yuri and Dimitri found their way into the military. Nikolai and I found a different path. We learned how to survive. When things changed, when democracy and capitalism came, we realized we were in a unique position to make money." Sighing slowly, he lifted his hands and tucked them behind his head. "But then I came here and found a way to get into some honest work."

"Fighting?"

He shook his head. "I never fought in any kind of professional match."

I frowned. "No?"

"I did my fighting in a different kind of cage."

"Oh." I glanced at his heavily scarred and tattooed hands. "*Oh*."

He nodded. "Word of mouth sold me as a trainer. A few winning fighters later and I had my business."

"But all this?" I gestured around his luxurious home. "It didn't come from fighting then?"

"No."

"Well then how did you make your money?"

Ivan dared to stroke my knee. His rough, callused palm rasped my skin. "It's better you don't ask that question."

His remark sent up a red flag but the sensation of his big, strong hand gliding over my leg left me unable to concentrate on it. All I could think about was the feeling of his warm skin on mine. I was so used to the soft hands of guys who worked in retail or office settings. There was something primal about Ivan's touch.

"Do I frighten you, Erin?" His fingertips trailed along my outer thigh.

I shivered under his feather-light touch. "Not really."

"No?"

I shook my head. "I think beneath all this," I gestured to his tattoos and scars, "you're probably the sweetest man I've ever met."

He snorted with amusement. "I wouldn't go that far."

"How far are you going to go?" It was a bold question to ask but I had to know.

"I don't know," he admitted quietly. His hand moved to my inner thigh but he didn't go higher than the bottom of the boxers. I sensed he warred with himself to keep his hand there, just there, and not any closer to that most intimate part of me.

Remembering our conversation at the gym, I asked, "Is this what you want for payment? For helping me?"

His gaze snapped to mine. The pained look on his face left me breathless. "No. I would never disrespect you in that way."

He started to pull his hand away but I squeezed my knees together and trapped it. My stomach wobbled with anticipation and excitement. "And what if I wanted you to?"

His lips twitched. "What if you wanted me to disrespect you?"

I thumped his forearm with my fingers. "You know what I mean. What if I wanted you?"

He grinned mischievously. "Wanted me to what?"

Now he was just playing with me. "Ivan..."

He sat forward and slid one muscled arm around my waist. His other hand cupped the back of my neck. Eye to eye with him, I held my breath. His heat and strength penetrated and enveloped me. Even with everything going on outside this room, I'd never felt safer.

"Be careful what you ask for, Erin," Ivan warned. "I'm not the kind of man to walk away from something I want." His thumb caressed the side of my neck. "One taste of you and I won't be able to let you go."

His warning did little to dissuade me. Instead I leaned forward and pressed my lips to his in a chaste kiss. A moment later, he growled, the sound so low and rumbling, that I shivered. Gathering me close, Ivan plundered my mouth, his tongue stabbing between my lips. I wound my arms around his neck and held on tight. He kissed me until I was dizzy and shuddering. Whatever concerns he'd harbored about getting involved with me were reduced to ashes by the passion flaming brightly between us.

I couldn't believe how different it felt to kiss Ivan. There was nothing awkward or uncertain in the way he captured my mouth, branding me with his insistent kisses. He knew what he wanted—and that was me. His skilled lips and tongue drove me wild as they ghosted along my jaw and down my neck. I cried out when he bit down gently on the fleshy spot where my neck curved into my collarbone. The sharp sensation traveled right down to my throbbing clit.

"Take this off," Ivan urged, his big hand jerking on the shirt I'd borrowed. "I have to see you. I have to touch you."

I grasped the bottom of the shirt and pulled it up and over my head. Ivan snatched away the shirt and tossed it on the floor. He stared at my naked breasts, his hungry gaze searing me and leaving me trembling. Those rough hands of his caressed my bare skin. He palmed my breasts and brushed his thumbs across my nipples. The dusky peaks drew tight to hard points.

"Ivan." I sighed his name as his lips skimmed my breast. He swirled his tongue around my nipple. The sensitive flesh responded instantly to his teasing licks.

IVAN

My breasts ached as arousal saturated my hot, fast pumping blood.

While he tormented my breasts with his mouth, I ran my hands over his buzzed scalp, the short hairs surprisingly soft against my palms. I'd had a handful of sexual experiences but none of them had been as electric and exciting as this one. No man had ever spent so much time stoking the flames of my arousal. Maybe that was why my other experiences paled in comparison to this one.

Ivan whispered something in Russian, his voice husky and thick. He must have seen the confusion on my face. He nuzzled my neck and captured my mouth in a sensual kiss that made my toes curl against his thighs. "You're beautiful. The most beautiful thing I've ever seen."

And he meant it. He wasn't simply flattering me to get into my pants. He actually thought I was that beautiful.

I touched my lips to his and reached for the buttons lining his shirt. My fingers faltered as I tried to kiss and unbutton at the same time. Coordination was clearly not my strong suit. Ivan chuckled against my mouth and gently swept my hands away from his chest. "Let me."

I watched as he peeled out of the shirt. Inch after delicious inch of unbelievably muscled and toned chest was revealed to me. I couldn't keep my hands off him. I ran my palms up and down his sexy pecs and washboard stomach. The crisp hair on his chest was something of a novelty for me. The tattoos and scars now fully revealed showed me just how much pain he'd known.

Giving in to the urge to kiss those old wounds, I leaned down and kissed the puckered scar that marked a spot just below his right shoulder. I knew what it was the moment I saw it. He'd been shot at some point in the past. I knew because Vivi had similar scars on her chest and another on her belly.

Ivan's sharp intake of breath accompanied the touch of my lips as they danced from one scar to another. His fingers sifted through my short hair. He tugged gently, silently urging me to lift my mouth. He claimed me in a passionate kiss. Eyes blazing with desire, he broke the kiss and pushed me down on the desk.

Flat on my back, I hissed as the cold wooden surface met my hot skin. A heartbeat later I hissed for another reason. Ivan's mouth dropped to my belly. He kissed and licked and nibbled his way right down to the waistband of the boxers I wore. With a couple of powerful jerks, he rid me of the boxers. Totally naked now, I licked my lips and waited.

IVAN

His mouth was on my leg now. He kissed his way up my calf before grasping both ankles and lifting my feet to the edge of the table. His hands cupped my inner thighs and pushed them gently apart. I held my breath at first, unable to draw even the smallest bit of air into my lungs as he petted my bare pussy.

"Oh!" I gasped as he parted the lips of my sex with his thick fingers. I closed my eyes and bit my lower lip as he carefully traced my pussy and slowly circled my clit. One big, long finger penetrated me, my slick nectar easing his entrance. I clawed at the desk in a desperate search for something to hold onto as he sensually teased me.

He whispered in Russian again, the words so alien to me but the meaning fully conveyed in his tone. He was fascinated by me. "I have to hear you come now."

"Ivan!" I cried out his name when his lips touched my pussy. I'd been on the receiving end of oral sex before but it had never felt like this. Ivan didn't attack my clit with fast strokes like my last boyfriend. No, he took his time exploring my pussy with his pliable tongue and avoided my clit.

He painted my entrance and nudged inside. My thighs tightened as the delicious sensation he evoked rocked me. He licked up one side of my labia and then the other before finally—finally!—letting his mouth drift toward my clit. He swirled his soft tongue around the pink pearl and suckled it gently. I arched up off the desk and moaned his name. "Ivan."

He groaned against my pussy and fluttered his tongue over the swollen bundle of nerves. I could feel myself growing wetter and wetter as that finger of his found its way inside me again. Thick and hard, it stroked shallow and slow at first. As the pace of his flicking against my clit hastened, so too did the pace and depth of the finger fucking me.

Ivan drove me crazy with his sensual assault. My lower belly burned and my thighs clenched and released. Curling my toes tightly against the desktop, I let my hand fall to his head and stroked his scalp as he ate me like a starving man. Never before had I gotten this close this fast. There was just something about Ivan that ignited my lust like no other.

"Please," I begged and scratched my nails against his scalp. "Please, Ivan."

He hummed against my clit and attacked the little bud with such fervor that I nearly passed out from sheer bliss. A flitting sensation of panic invaded my core. A split-second later, I came hard. His tongue lashed my pussy. Muscles tense and nipples pulsing, I rode the waves of ecstasy. "Ivan! Ivan! *Ah!*"

As my climax faded, Ivan's tongue stabbed into my wet pussy. I clapped a hand over my mouth to muffle a shriek. His fingers bit into the supple flesh of my inner thighs as he feasted on my pussy. While his tongue plunged into me again and again, he strummed my clit with his thumb. Bliss coiled low and tight in my belly until, finally, the tension snapped and I came a second time. Head thrown back, I moaned against my palm and tried not to screech with sheer delight.

Just when I thought I might pass out, Ivan showed mercy. He gently wiped his mouth on my inner thigh and kissed my mound. A moment later, he shocked me by pulling me off the desk and right onto his lap. I stifled a gasp and stiffened at the sudden burn of his body heat as my breasts touched his chest.

"Easy," he urged gently, his lips so close to my ear. "I've got you."

Oh yes he did. There was just enough space in the roomy office chair for my knees to fit on either side of his thighs. "Ivan..."

When he kissed me this time, I could taste myself on him. The heady, intimate experience left me dizzy. My pussy ached to be filled by him. I gripped his strong shoulders. "I need you, Ivan. I need you inside me."

"We can't," he said with a growl. "I don't have any condoms."

The insertion of reality jarred me. Still, I wasn't about to let this perfect moment pass. "I'm on the pill."

He chuckled. "Don't tempt me, Erin."

I wiggled my naked ass and reached between our bodies to grasp his erection through the tented fabric of his pants. Smiling, I reminded him, "That's the whole point, Ivan."

With a strangled groan of reluctance, Ivan grabbed my hand. "I won't risk it. I'm clean, of course, but that's not the big issue."

Even through the dense haze of lust clouding my judgment I understood what he meant. We hardly knew one another. One moment of passion could lead to a lifetime as parents. That was a step we definitely weren't ready to take.

"Then let me touch you." I brushed my knuckles over his erection. "Let me make you feel good."

"You already make me feel good," he assured me. I detected the barest hint of frustration in his voice, almost as if he didn't want me to have that power over him. Even so, he reached down and unbuttoned his pants. I pushed his hands out of the way and lowered the zipper. The bulge in his black boxer briefs drew my attention.

"Oh my god," I whispered in awe. "You're huge."

Ivan laughed. "You don't have to flatter me, Erin. I've already opened my pants to you."

"I wasn't flattering you." My gaze fell to his lap. As if unwrapping a package on Christmas morning, I slowly peeled down the front of his boxer briefs. His massive cock sprang free. Long and thick, it throbbed beneath my fingertips. Shiny droplets of pre-cum oozed from the tip. I gathered them with my thumb and brought the slick wetness to my tongue. Ivan's nostrils flared as I licked his seed from my skin. "Delicious."

"Are you always such a dirty girl?" he wondered softly.

I shook my head and brushed my lips against his. "Only for you, Ivan."

As our tongues dueled, I reached down and grasped him with both hands. I stroked him at a leisurely pace. There was no reason to rush. His velvety skin covered such steely heat. Holding his big cock in my hands, I had to wonder if I could take him when the time came. None of my boyfriends had ever come close to this. What would it feel like? Amazing, no doubt.

Ivan's heavy breaths buffeted my cheek. His hand moved between my open thighs. He caressed my slit, rubbing his fingertips over my clit before plunging two fingers deep inside my pussy. I gasped against his mouth.

Eye to eye, we didn't say one word. Hearts racing, we communicated with staccato breaths and shallow pants. My fingers tightened around his rigid shaft. His curved inside my slick channel. Gyrating on his lap, I rode his fingers. He lifted his hips to meet the downward strokes of my hands. His lips danced across my collarbone and drifted toward my breast. When his thumb moved to the side of my clit, the pressure was just enough to send me hurtling over the edge into the abyss of ecstasy.

Ivan buried his face against my neck as I came and grunted my name. "Erin!"

A split-second later, I felt the first hot splash of semen on my belly. We clutched and jerked in the chair as we shuddered in the grips of our shared climax. I stroked him until he trembled and the last bit of cum had been milked from his cock. Forehead to forehead, we panted and held onto one another.

In that moment, nothing outside the walls of his office existed. There was no Ruby, no Andrei, no Albanian mob or Hermanos street gang. It was just the two of us—and it was perfect.

Ivan caressed my cheek. "Erin, I—"

The shrill ring of a phone interrupted him. Frowning in annoyance, he reached for the cell phone rattling across his desk. He answered gruffly in Russian. I spotted the instant change in his demeanor. Whatever was being said wasn't good. My gut clenched and I waited to hear the worst.

Ivan couldn't believe someone was calling right now. Erin had the sweetest, most tender look on her face. His cum was still wet on her belly. He needed to tell her that she meant something to him, that this wasn't simply a quick fuck to him.

Irritated, he grabbed the phone and answered. "Yes?"

"Ivan." Yuri's familiar voice filtered out of the speaker. He was barely audible over the thumping bass of music in the background. No doubt he was in the VIP section of one of his sleek, ultra popular clubs. "I found something you've lost."

He instantly perked up. "And what's that?"

"A certain limping fighter just tried to sell his cheap shit in my bathroom," Yuri said, his voice laced with disgust. "The bouncers tossed his ass onto the street before I realized who he was. He can't have gone far."

Ivan knew Yuri wasn't about to send one of his own men after Andrei. He'd never put them in the crossfire of the Albanians or the Hermanos. "I'm send-ing Dimitri."

"I hope you know what you're doing."

"I do."

"Is she very pretty?" There was no mistaking the amusement in Yuri's voice.

Ivan frowned. How the hell did Yuri know about Erin? "Nikolai?"

Yuri laughed. "Who else?"

Ivan glanced at Erin who looked perplexed. It occurred to him that she couldn't understand what he was saying. Even with that confused expression on her face, she was still the loveliest thing he'd ever seen. "Yes, she is."

"I'm glad to hear it. I'd hate to think you were risking everything for anything less."

Yuri's subtle warning came through clearly. Of their tight-knit group, Yuri had always been the most cautious and conservative. Undoubtedly that had been the secret to the multi-billion dollar fortune he'd amassed in oil and minerals.

"Thanks for the tip. I'll see you around."

"Be careful, Ivan."

He ended the call and pulled up Dimitri's number. As he waited for his friend to answer, he held Erin's concerned gaze. "We've found Andrei."

4 CHAPTER FOUR

My stomach churned with anxiety as Kostya navigated the heavy night traffic. I glanced at Ivan who sat in the front seat and wished he was back here with me. After what we'd shared in his office, I felt our connection more than ever and craved his heat and strength. If Ivan's friend was right about Andrei, Ruby might finally be within grasp.

When Ivan's cell phone rang, my ears perked. I held my breath as he talked in rapid-fire Russian. A few seconds later, he hung up and barked instructions at Kostya. The SUV switched lanes and made an unexpected turn. Before I could ask what was happening, Ivan looked back at me.

"Dimitri missed Andrei by a few minutes but he found someone else who knows Ruby. She's at a crack house across town. Dimitri is taking the kid with him to find her but we'll probably beat them."

I nodded and swallowed hard. My hands balled into fists on my lap. If Ruby was alone again, she was a prime target for both of the vicious gangs hunting her. I closed my eyes and prayed we'd get there first.

Within twenty minutes, we were driving the rough streets of one of Houston's more blighted neighborhoods. Broken-down cars sat in the front yards of ramshackle houses. There were few windows that weren't boarded up and covered in graffiti. Most of the houses looked unoccupied. There were only a handful of lights to be seen on the empty streets.

"Erin."

Ivan's firm voice drew my gaze. "Yes?"

"You will stay behind me. If I tell you to get back in the vehicle, you go. Understood?"

"Yes." After my narrow escape at the last crack house, I wasn't keen on repeating the experience.

As the SUV crawled to a stop along the cracked sidewalk, another pair of headlights came into view. The other vehicle, this one a silver truck, parked across the street from us. I recognized the man who climbed out of the driver's seat from the gym. Tall and blond, he sported the classic Russian look. His hawk-like gaze scanned the street before he gestured to the person riding in his front seat.

The young man who came around the front of the truck surprised me. The Latino boy wore a stark white wife-beater and low slung jeans and held tight to his waistband. There was no missing the dark black gang insignia tattooed across his neck.

Kostya mumbled something to Ivan who grunted. Curious, I glanced at him but Ivan shook his head. Whatever the story, I wasn't getting it tonight.

Out on the sidewalk, I fought the urge to run into the house and frantically search for Ruby. Dimitri and the young man joined us. Kostya hung back, his shoulders pressed against the driver's door as he watched the street like some kind of sentry guard.

"Johnny says he saw Ruby and Andrei here earlier." Dimitri gripped the young man's shoulder tightly. The high-school aged kid winced. "Apparently, the Hermanos have a flop house a few streets over. Johnny supplies the place with stolen booze and drugs to keep the whores happy." Dimitri's gaze fell on me. "He says your sister went there looking for work."

My stomach lurched painfully. Ruby a prostitute? As if sensing my horror, Ivan gently rubbed the small of my back. Compassion flashed across his harsh face.

"She didn't stay," Johnny said, his voice low and soft. "When she realized who the house belonged to, she ran. I was worried she was going to get hit by a car or something so I followed her back here. She was in a bad way. I tried to get her to come with me but she was really confused and asking for a guy named Aaron."

"No, it's Erin. That's me."

"Oh." He looked a bit sheepish. "Well I tried to help her but then her boyfriend came back and I realized who he was so I got the hell out of there. I was going to tell my crew I'd Andrei." Johnny hesitated. "But then I heard that Dimitri and his crew were looking for the girlfriend and I thought maybe she'd be safer with him than out here with a big fucking target on her back."

His kindness surprised me. "Why did you want to help her?"

Johnny lowered his gaze. His jaw tightened. "I've got a sister."

I understood then. Looking to Ivan, I asked, "Can we go in now?"

"Hey, man," Johnny addressed Dimitri, "that place is packed with tweakers. They're all fucked out of their heads. You don't want to just go busting in there. One of those methheads might think you're a cop and pop your Russian ass."

"Then maybe I should send you through the door first." Dimitri pulled a flashlight from one back pocket. I spotted the outline of a pistol under his thin jacket. He glanced at Johnny and pointed at the truck. "Go. Now."

The kid nodded but I had a feeling he was going to run the second Dimitri's back was turned. With Dimitri leading the way and Ivan two steps behind, I followed the pair into the house. Once inside, the overpowering stench hit me. The putrid mix smelled of piss and so much more. I put a hand to my mouth and tried not to gag. How the hell could Ruby stand a place like this?

My eyes widened as Dimitri's flashlight beam bounced around the cramped rooms of the small house. There were bodies littering couches and the floor. A television blared a late show, the crowd's applause deafening as it ricocheted off the walls. Two faces turned our way but the two men seemed unable to focus. Their bleary-eyed gazes turned back to the television.

In the kitchen, one man was slumped over a table. A stark naked woman stood in front of the fridge and scribbled aimlessly on the once-white surface with a black marker. She mumbled incoherently. I couldn't drag my gaze away from the bizarre markings she'd placed on her bare skin.

Ivan grasped my hand and tugged me along. He brought a finger to his mouth, urging me to be quiet and keep moving forward. Dimitri popped into one bedroom but came out quickly. Shaking his head, he pointed to another door. This one Ivan opened. I peered around his brawny arm—and discovered Ruby.

"Oh god!" Terrified by the sight of my sister sprawled on the floor, I squeezed by Ivan and into the room. I started to kneel next to her but Ivan grasped me by the waist and lifted me up. He used his shoe to kick aside the dirty syringe I hadn't seen.

With an admonishing frown, he whispered, "Careful!"

"Sorry." Glancing around, I found a clean spot to kneel and gently rolled Ruby onto her side. Vomit smeared her face and speckled her hair. Urine soaked the carpet and her dirty clothing. Her cold, clammy skin scared me. I tried to find her pulse but my fingers slipped in the sweaty grime coating her skin. I bent my face and pressed my ear to her chest. Her fast, weak heartbeat filled me with hope. "She's still alive! Call 9-1-1!"

"No." Ivan denied my request. "There isn't enough time."

I sat back on my heels as Ivan crouched down and scooped Ruby into his arms. "But we passed a fire station—"

IVAN

Ivan shot me a look and I finally understood. Our arrival to this house wouldn't have gone unnoticed in this neighborhood. We were sitting ducks.

"Erin. Go!"

I jumped to my feet and ran to the front door. Ivan, his arms burdened with my sister's unconscious body, shadowed me to the front door. Dimitri followed us onto the sidewalk. He cursed loudly upon realizing Johnny had fled while were inside.

Ivan growled at Dimitri in Russian but whatever Dimitri snarled back shut Ivan right up. Not wanting to get involved in their squabble, I rushed to the SUV and jumped into the middle seat. I grabbed Ruby's shoulders and dragged her onto my lap with Ivan's help. He slipped onto the other end of the bench seat and draped her legs across his.

"Seatbelt, Erin." Even with chaos swirling around us, Ivan's sole concern was my safety. I quickly grabbed my belt and jammed it into place.

Kostya didn't even need to be told what to do. He buckled up and punched the gas. We screeched out of there like a bat out of hell. Dimitri's truck followed close behind but I couldn't think about the risk of the Hermanos or Albanians catching up with us now.

My fingertips drifted to Ruby's neck. I found her pulse and kept my fingers there. The fast blips reassured me. This wasn't the first time she'd overdosed but I'd never seen one this bad. It occurred to me that I had no idea what she'd taken or how much. I prayed the emergency room staff would be able to save her.

"Look at me, *angel moy.*" Ivan's stern voice infiltrated my fearful thoughts. He reached over and touched my face. The searing sweep of his fingertips reassured me. "It's going to be okay."

Because Ivan said it, I believed it.

The sun had just started to peek over the horizon when Ivan made his way out of the hospital to a bench near the smoking area. He fished his phone from his pocket and started making phone calls. There was no way he'd make it into the gym at his usual early hour. He'd rely on the other trainers to open up and get his fighters moving through their morning routines.

As he was finishing up his conversation with Paco, Ivan spotted Dimitri crossing the parking lot. His old friend carried two cups of coffee and a bright yellow bag stamped with the red logo of that Mexican bakery Dimitri lived above. Even though his friend had more than enough money to buy his own place, he stayed there in that cramped apartment. He swore it was the hot breakfast that kept him hanging around but Ivan suspected it was more likely the pretty dark-haired young woman who worked behind the counter...

"I thought you two could use some breakfast." Dimitri shook the bag. "They're still warm."

Ivan accepted the coffee and paper bag. A pang of guilt soured his gut as he remembered the awful thing he'd shouted at Dimitri when'd emerged from the house to find Johnny gone. He eyed Dimitri carefully. "Look, about the boy last night—"

Dimitri cut him off with a slash of his hand. "We're not talking about Johnny."

"We are." Ivan pinned his friend with a determined gaze. "I've been thinking about what I said to you and it was wrong of me. I didn't..." Ivan's voice trailed off and he glanced at the hospital. "I know I've been riding your ass about getting involved with the bakery girl, especially since her kid brother is up to his eyeballs in shit with the Hermanos, but I understand it now."

Dimitri's expression faltered. Finally, he said, "I'm not involved with Benny. I'm just her tenant. That's it."

Ivan wasn't so sure about that but he wasn't about to pry into his friend's private life.

"How's the sister?"

"Not good," Ivan said, his thoughts turning to Erin's distraught face.

Never one to ease into difficult conversations, Dimitri said, "Erin is still in danger. What are you going to do?"

"I don't know yet," Ivan admitted. "I'll bounce some ideas off Nikolai but he made it perfectly clear yesterday that he doesn't want to get dragged into this."

"I'll look for Andrei. Maybe we can do a trade of some kind."

Ivan held Dimitri's hardened gaze. The unspoken words hung in the air between them. "It wouldn't be very clean."

Dimitri shrugged. "These kinds of horse trades rarely are but maybe if we can give them Andrei and some money, they'll leave Erin and her sister alone."

His chest tightened with the realization that such an ugly decision loomed on the horizon. "Find Andrei."

"On it."

He watched Dimitri cross the parking lot before heading back into the hospital. As he made his way up to the private room where they'd moved Ruby, Ivan scanned his surroundings. The small crowds in the waiting areas and huddled around the elevators drew his attention. It would be easy for either of the gangs after Ruby to send someone into the hospital to finish her off or pump her for information on Andrei and the money and the drugs. Ivan doubted she knew anything. From the state of the shithole she'd been left in by Andrei, the man didn't value her very highly. Maybe he'd decided to cut his losses and leave her behind for the gangs as a twisted kind of peace offering.

Ivan paused in the open doorway of Ruby's room. Pale and bruised, Ruby reclined in the hospital bed. Wires and tubes snaked from her thin, frail body. She desperately needed a bath and a good meal.

Erin sat in a chair next to the bed. She'd finally fallen asleep. Not wanting to wake her, he entered the room as quietly as possible and placed the breakfast items on a rolling tray against the wall. He lowered himself into a chair next to Erin and sipped the strong black coffee.

Unable to help himself, Ivan put the cup of coffee on the floor and gently took her small hand in his. The simple act of touching her soft skin calmed his raw nerves. He couldn't shake the notion that he was falling fast—too fast—for Erin but there it was.

Like a siren, she called to him, enchanting and binding him to her. There was nothing he wouldn't do for her. Taking on two vicious gangs and a drug addict sister seemed a low price to pay for keeping Erin in his life.

It wasn't simply her beautiful face or the shockingly hot sex they'd shared that made him want her. Those things were nice, of course, but the intense pull he felt toward Erin came from a different place. She was something sweet and pure that demanded protection. She'd put her trust in him and he would never allow her to regret that. As long as she wanted him, he would protect and defend her.

Erin stirred. She inhaled a long, slow breath and blinked a few times. Her gaze jumped around the room. A grimace tugged at the corners of her mouth. When she glanced at him, her expression softened. Her lips curved in a smile. "Ivan."

Knowing that his presence put her at ease filled him with such happiness. Ivan swept his fingers down her face. "I didn't mean to wake you."

She looked down to their joined hands and gave his a squeeze. "I don't mind." Looking a bit bashful, she admitted, "I liked waking up to find you here, holding my hand."

There was so much Ivan wanted to say but this wasn't the place. Things were good between them right now. He was content to leave it until later. "Dimitri brought you something to eat. Are you hungry?"

She nodded. "Starving, actually."

He doubted that very much but didn't correct her. People here flung around the word so lightly but none of them knew real starvation, not as he and his friends had as children.

Ivan untangled their hands and rose from his chair. He grabbed the bag of pastries and the other cup of coffee. She took them with a smile. "Right after you left, I had a chance to speak with a nurse. She said Ruby will probably drift in and out of sleep all day."

He returned to his seat and picked up his coffee. "I'm not surprised. A human body can't take that much abuse. She's lucky to be alive."

Erin peeled a soft bit of bread from the brightly iced bun. She nibbled it slowly. "I think she wanted to die."

His gaze snapped to Erin's face. She looked so sad and he ached for her. "I don't—"

"No." She interrupted him with an anguished frown. "You don't know her. She's never taken that much or tried so many different kinds of drugs in such a short time period." Erin stared at her sister. "I think she was afraid the gangs were going to catch up with her and decided that was the best way out of the mess."

Ivan didn't know what to say. He didn't want to upset her anymore so he tried to find a gentle reply to set her at ease. "Let's be happy that she's alive. All the rest? It doesn't matter. Not now."

Erin seemed content with that piece of advice. She quietly finished her breakfast while he stroked her arm and upper back. When she was done, Erin turned her full attention to him. "You found Ruby."

He nodded. "I did."

"That was our deal. You'd help me find Ruby. So what happens now? With us, I mean."

He heard the anxiety in her voice. "What do you want?"

"You."

It was a simple answer but one so powerful. Wanting to soothe her nerves, he leaned over and brushed his lips across her cheek. "Then you've got me."

She grasped his hand and tugged him closer for a proper kiss. More seriously, she asked, "And what about the gangs after Ruby?"

"Don't you worry about that. I'll protect you, *angel moy*."

5 CHAPTER FIVE

Sometime later, I found myself alone with Ruby. Lena and Vivi had stopped by for a little while to bring me some clean clothes and an overnight bag. Trading emergency keys with my closest friends had been a good idea after all. Vivi had wanted to stay but Lena had rightly guessed that I needed some time alone with Ruby. Just knowing my two best friends were there for me was more than enough.

Ivan's absence from the hospital I felt more keenly. He'd finally left around noon when I'd forced him to go. The man needed a nap and a shower and a good meal. Still I couldn't deny that his hesitation to leave me hadn't touched me deeply. It had been a long time since I'd had a strong man in my life or someone who wanted to protect and care for me. What Ivan seemed to be offering tempted me a great deal.

But I couldn't think about my love life right now. Ruby still hadn't become totally conscious. She'd wake for a few seconds and then fall right back asleep. I found the steady beep of the heart monitor reassuring. It let me know that she was doing much better than she looked.

The sight of so much grime and dirt on Ruby made my skin crawl. I found the stack of washcloths and the towels the kind nurse had left me. I filled a blue plastic basin with some warm water and some of the liquid soap in the toiletry kit provided.

After swishing around the mixture with my fingers, I carried it to the rolling cart and moved it next to the bed. I dipped a washcloth in the soapy water, wrung it out and gently wiped her arm and hand. Slowly, I moved around the bed, cleaning the skin exposed by her loose-fitting hospital gown. Hopefully she'd be strong enough to stand up for a shower later but this was the best I could do right now.

As I dabbed at her sticky face, Ruby moaned. She began to wake. Obviously groggy, she blinked rapidly and glanced around the hospital room. I smiled at her and brushed the washcloth over her cheek to wipe away some of the filth clinging to her skin. "Hey, sleepyhead."

Instead of a smile, I received a nasty glare. Her voice gravelly, Ruby asked, "What the hell am I doing here?"

I steeled myself for the inevitable ugliness. When she came down from a high, Ruby could be a real monster. Calmly, I explained, "You overdosed last night. We brought you to the hospital."

"Why?" She tried to sit up but fell back.

Not wanting to see her struggle, I reached for the bed remote and carefully adjusted the head of the bed. I fluffed the pillow behind her and tried to help her into a more comfortable position but she fought me. "You were sick and I thought you were going to die. That's why you're in a hospital."

"Oh please," she growled. "Spare me the love bull-shit."

I coiled the remote cord around the bed rail. "It's not bullshit, Ruby. You're my sister. I love you."

"Then where the hell were you when I called you begging for help?"

"What are you talking about? I came to get you but you weren't there."

"If you really loved me, you would have gotten there faster."

I bit my tongue. She was probably in pain and desperate for a fix. "I drove as fast possible."

"Well not fast enough!" Ruby huffed and jerked at the thin sheet covering her. "Andrei came back but he didn't want to wait for you. He said you weren't going to come and he was right."

I fought the urge to roll my eyes and remind her just what a prize Andrei was. "Look, I did the best I could to get there. I'm sorry that we missed each other but it was probably for the best. A bunch of scary guys found me there when I arrived."

Ruby's eyes narrowed. "Oh and I'm sure that's my fault!"

"Well—yeah, it is."

"Sure, Erin, just throw it in my face that I'm such a fuck up!"

"I didn't say that." I reached for her hand but she snatched it away.

"Don't touch me!"

"Okay." I backed away from the bed. It was easy to recognize the signs that she was about to explode. It wouldn't have been the first time she'd flown at me in a drug-induced rage. "You just need to rest."

"Don't tell me what to do." She tightly gripped the sheet. "You're always telling me what to do."

"I don't think that's fair, Ruby. I'm always telling you not to do drugs and not to steal and not to lie to doctors. It's hardly the same thing as ordering you around for some kind of sick, twisted pleasure."

"You're such a bitch." Her snarled reply hit me hard. "You think you're so fucking perfect with your stupid job and your stupid school and your stupid friends. You know what you are? You're a lonely, miserable freak. At least I have a man who loves me."

Loves you enough to drag you into a gang war and abandon you in a crack house. I squashed the nasty thought and grabbed my purse and the small overnight bag. Certain we were going to get into a real fight, I headed for the open door. "I don't have to listen to this crap, Ruby."

"Oh yeah! Just leave! Go on! Walk out on me like everyone else!"

I turned around to tell her that no one had ever walked out on her but saw the plastic basin flying at my head. I moved at the last second. The basin slammed into the wall. All the dirty water it held soaked me.

Gasping with shock and indignation, I demanded, "What the hell is wrong with you?"

"Fuck you, Erin. Get out! Get. Out."

"Gladly." Face burning with humiliation, I stepped out of the room—and ran right into Dimitri. "Sorry."

Ivan's tall, blond friend gazed down at me with such concern. "It's fine. Are you okay?"

From inside the hospital room, Ruby continued to berate me with a string of filthy words. Tears stung my eyes at her awful treatment of me. Logically, I knew it was the drugs making her this way but it didn't make it hurt any less.

Dimitri shrugged out of his thin gray jacket and draped it around me shoulders. "We're leaving."

"Erin! Come back! I'm sorry. Please! I'm sorry!" Ruby's pitiful pleading echoed in the hallway.

I glanced at the open door and the nurses rushing in to deal with Ruby. "I should stay."

"I wasn't asking. You're coming home to Ivan." Dimitri glared at Ruby's room where such a ruckus now erupted. "He wouldn't allow that woman to talk to you like that if he was here—and I won't either. You don't deserve that kind of abuse."

"She's sick."

"She's a junkie. She did this to herself."

"Please," I begged softly. "Don't say that."

His hard expression lost some of its edge but he didn't apologize. "Come on."

There was no use fighting him. Part of me knew Dimitri was right. My presence was only going to agitate Ruby. She needed to rest and heal, not fight with me over imagined slights.

As we made our way to the nurses' station, I heard Ruby screaming such terrible things at the nurses and doctors trying to tend her. My face flamed with embarrassment but the sweet nurse at the desk assured me they were used to dealing with this kind of thing. It didn't make me feel any better. It actually made me feel really bad for the hospital staff who had to put up with that type of crap day in and day out.

After being assured I would be contacted if Ruby's condition changed and that a social worker and counselor were on their way to speak with her, I let Dimitri lead me out of the hospital. He unlocked the passenger side door and waited for me to climb up into the cab before shutting it firmly.

"Would you like to grab something to eat on the way back to Ivan's?" Dimitri started the truck and backed out of the parking space.

"Why are you taking me to Ivan's? Why can't I just go home?"

He glanced at me and frowned. "It's not safe."

"If it's not safe for me to go home, it's not safe for Ruby to be left at the hospital."

"She's being watched. You don't need to worry about her. I have instructions to take you back to Ivan so that's what I'm going to do."

I bristled at the idea that Ivan had simply made all these decisions without even consulting me. I understood why he'd done it. He took my safety very seriously but I wanted to be asked for my opinion. Staring out the window, I figured this was going to be the topic of our first argument as a couple.

A couple.

The idea didn't frighten me as much as it should have. I'd always been timid about men and relationships, always afraid to take chances, but with Ivan I felt none of that. Deep down inside, I recognized that he was something special. The connection we shared was unique and worth pursuing.

"So?"

Dimitri's question drew my gaze. "So what?"

He chuckled and shook his head. "Did you want to hit up a drive-thru or not?"

"Oh! Yes."

We settled on my favorite burger chain. As we waited in line, I finally worked up the courage to ask him something that had been nagging me all day. "How do you know that Johnny guy?"

Dimitri studied me for an unnervingly long moment. "He's the younger brother of my landlady."

I hadn't been expecting that. "I see."

"Benny took over her family's bakery last year but I've lived upstairs for nearly five years. Her grandmother let me rent the place cheaply in exchange for certain services. When she died, I decided to stay. It's a nice place. The rent is cheap."

"Services?" I considered what I knew of Dimitri. He didn't strike me as the type of man I'd want to cross. "You keep the place safe?"

He nodded. "It used to be a vibrant neighborhood but it's going through some growing pains. I make sure no one tries to strong arm the bakery into paying protection fees or taxes on deliveries."

"Jesus," I said softly. "I had no idea it was that much of a headache to run a bakery."

"You'd be surprised," he muttered. "People can get nasty when it comes to greed and money."

"And this Johnny? He's in the Hermanos gang?" I touched my neck. "I saw the tattoos he had."

Dimitri scowled as he let his foot off the brake and eased his truck forward in the line. "He's a dumbass kid who thinks being part of a gang makes him tough. He has no idea what kind of mistake he's making."

"But you do?" The words left my mouth before I could stop them.

Dimitri's jaw tightened. "We're done talking about me."

My eyes widened at his gruff reply. "Okay."

He exhaled a little roughly. "I'm not angry with you. Please don't misunderstand me."

"I get it. We're fine."

And we were. I'd gone too far in my questioning and he'd shut me down. It was that simple and didn't hurt my feelings.

By the time we reached Ivan's house, I was starting to feel the effects of my long night and eventful day. I took my lunch upstairs to the guest room and stripped out of my clothes for a quick hot shower. Clean and sleepy, I slipped into one of the sleeping shirts my friends had packed and scarfed down my lunch.

With a full belly and an aching head, I climbed into bed and hugged a pillow. My gaze settled on my phone. I'd left it on the bedside table, just in case the hospital tried to call me. Right now, I desperately wanted to call Ivan but couldn't work up the courage. Somehow I didn't think listening to me whine for an hour was a good way to start our relationship.

In the end, I decided not to chance it. All those confusing emotions and conflicted thoughts could wait. My eyelids drifted together and I succumbed to exhaustion and the blissful pull of sleep.

Hours later, I came awake to the sensation of being watched. The sheet was twisted around my hips and thighs. Apparently I hadn't found the peaceful respite I so desperately needed. After a little tugging, I got free from the sheet and pushed up into a sitting position.

IVAN

"I'm sorry." Ivan's rumbling voice pierced the darkness. "I didn't mean to wake you."

My gaze finally found him. He stood in the doorway of the room, his silhouette dark against the light from the hallway. "I don't mind."

He chuckled softly. "No, I didn't think you would."

"Is it late?"

"It's nearly nine. I tried to get here sooner but kept getting sidetracked. I was surprised you didn't call me."

"I wanted to," I admitted, "but I wasn't sure you wanted to listen to me cry about Ruby."

"I wouldn't have minded."

Feeling a bit nervous and glad for the shadows that hid my face, I asked, "Will you stay with me tonight?"

Quietly, he stepped into the room and shut the door behind him. The room was totally dark except for the small bit of moonlight streaming through the window. He made his way to the bed and switched on the lamp there. The soft, dim glow gave off just enough light. I watched him toe off his shoes and shed his clothing. He left on his boxer briefs before lifting the cover and sliding in next to me.

Though he'd seen me naked last night, this was the most I'd seen of him. His tattooed skin tantalized me. When he reached for me, I went willingly. His strong arms hauled me close. Gently, he pressed me onto my back and slid down onto his side. He caressed my face with his callused, scarred hands and gazed down at me with such tenderness.

"I'm sorry your sister was so ugly with you." He brushed his lips across my mouth. "You didn't deserve that."

No doubt Dimitri had given him a blow-by-blow of my dust-up with Ruby. "She's just sick and in pain."

"That doesn't give her the right to make you her punching bag."

"No," I agreed and rubbed my hands up and down his muscled biceps. His hot skin awakened my desire. I lifted up to meet his mouth. He claimed me with a kiss so intensely sensual that my lower belly flip-flopped. "Ivan..."

He traced my jaw. "We don't have to do anything tonight. I'm happy to hold you if that's all you want."

The strangest sensation of rightness settled over me as I stared into his light blue eyes. Beneath that mean looking exterior existed the sweetest, gentlest man I'd ever known—and all he wanted to do was hold me. No man had ever just wanted to hold me. There was always some other motive to the cuddling but not with Ivan.

As much as I appreciated his offer, it wasn't what I wanted. Not tonight, at least.

IVAN

Caressing the back of his neck, I whispered, "Make love to me. Make me feel something other than worry and guilt."

He nuzzled my cheek and ghosted his lips across my ear. "I'll make you forget. I'll make it good for you."

Of that I had no doubt.

Ivan's kisses left me dizzy and breathless. I ran my hands up and down his broad back, feeling the hard muscle beneath his surprisingly soft skin. His tongue plundered my mouth. The way he took possession of me made my fingers tremble. How he'd learned the secrets to my body so quickly confounded me.

Unlike last night, when we'd come together in a rush of lust and need, we took a leisurely approach. Ivan's rough hands slipped under the thin fabric of my night shirt. He peeled it off my body and tossed it onto the floor. Naked beneath him, I purred with delight as his searching hands and teasing mouth moved over my bare skin.

His tongue laved my nipples. The dusky buds formed tight peaks that he pinched and rolled between his fingertips. I rose up on my shoulders, arching my back from the sheer torment of being so sensually tweaked. He eased the pinching bite of his fingertips with his wet tongue, circling and sucking my nipples until I was groaning and gripping his sides.

With my legs wrapped around his waist, I could feel the hot, hard length of him jutting into my belly. His boxer briefs were so tented by his huge cock that the waistband no longer touched that plane of skin below his navel. I couldn't wait to get my hands on him and reached down between our bodies to grasp his steely shaft. Ivan grunted with pleasure and captured my mouth again.

"Please tell me you have condoms." I couldn't imagine being denied the sensation of his cock buried inside me another night.

"I do," he said with a laugh. "In my pocket. I stopped at the store on the way home, just in case."

"Oh thank god!" I giggled and kissed him. "I want to feel you inside me so badly."

"Not yet," he murmured and grazed his lips down the curve of my throat.

I shuddered as his mouth skimmed my body. He kissed a ticklish trail from my neck to my navel before throwing back the sheet and comforter and shoving my thighs wide apart. I rose up on my elbows to watch him parting the lips of my sex. The sight of this big, strong man between my thighs left me quivering.

"Ivan!" I cried out his name and fell back to the bed when his tongue finally touched my throbbing clit. He nibbled the pink bud before flicking it a few times. When he suckled that tender pearl, I thrashed wildly.

IVAN

His tongue fluttered over the swollen bud, expertly pushing me closer and closer to the edge. My thighs were pushed even wider apart, forcing me open to his oral assault.

I came with a strangled groan. My hips rocked off the bed but he held me firmly in place, lashing my pussy with his tongue until I climaxed a second time. The hard, fast orgasm made my heart race and my belly clench. Gripped by the waves of pleasure, I panted and shook when he was done with me.

He kissed my mound and lower belly before sliding over to the edge of the mattress and reaching down for his pants. When he'd retrieved a condom, he shed the last piece of clothing covering him and pushed up onto his knees. I licked my lips and watched with fascination as he stroked his long, hard cock in his big hand. He tore open the package and tossed it onto the floor. His fingers rolled the condom down his shaft.

When he moved over me, I experienced a thrill of excitement. He planted his hands on either side of my head. Our noses touched and then he kissed me, drawing out the sensual mating of our mouths. I wound my arms around him and clutched his shoulders. He broke away from my mouth and caressed my cheek while whispering in Russian. I didn't need to speak his language to understand what he was saying to me.

His cock nudged my pussy and his punishing kisses drove the air right out of my lungs. With one rough thrust, he entered me completely. I gasped at the sudden intrusion. His long, thick dick filled and stretched me. "Ivan!"

He kissed me tenderly and rocked slowly in and out of me. My slick wetness eased his way as his cock retreated almost completely before plunging forward again. The intimate joining of our bodies felt unlike anything I'd ever experienced. Pinned beneath Ivan's hot, strong body, I felt completely owned and incredibly secure. There was no other place I wanted to be than right here.

I grasped his shoulders and responded to his snapping hips by rising up to meet his deep, hard strokes. Gripping and clutching, we moved together atop the bed. Ivan awoke such fiery need within me. I couldn't get enough of him. Saturated with desire, I relished the vibrant sensations rippling through me.

Ivan shifted above me. One of his hands moved down between our bodies. I moaned loudly when his fingers found my clit. He tapped the little bundle of nerves, eliciting a sharp gasp from my throat. He chuckled with amusement and fucked me harder and faster. His fingertip swirled in the wetness coating the swollen bundle of nerves. My thighs tightened around his waist. Coils of bliss unfurled in my belly and spread through my core.

"Please," I begged, my pussy throbbing and clit aching. "Please, Ivan."

"Come for me," he ordered, his voice so gruff and demanding. "Come now, Erin."

With a cry of passion, I shattered beneath him. The climax stole my breath but his playful nip on my exposed collarbone forced me to inhale. His fingers circled and stimulated me until I was pleading with him to stop. "Oh god! No more. I can't...*ah!*"

He claimed my mouth with a searing kiss but showed mercy by abandoning my clitoris. Growling with desire, he grasped both my wrists in one massive paw and dragged them up over my head. He held them in place and began to fuck me like some feral beast. His cock slammed into me again and again.

Head thrown back, I cried his name over and over while he ravished me. The bed rattled beneath us, the headboard slamming into the wall with such force that I was sure he was going to need to call in a crew for repairs. Sex had never been like this for me. It was wild and wicked and ever so good. His body brushed against mine in just the right way. In no time at all, I hovered on the verge of coming again—and he knew it.

All it took was one subtle shift of his hips and I shrieked with pleasure. Ivan groaned as my pussy clenched him in time with the rhythmic bursts of delight coursing through me. His jerky thrusts and grunting sigh of my name heralded his release. As we clutched and shuddered together, his forehead touched mine.

When he finally pulled away from me, I was sad to feel the loss of his heat and his weight. Ivan brushed his lips over mine before sliding out of bed and walking to the bathroom. I rolled onto my side and enjoyed the view of his taut ass and tattooed back before he disappeared.

The necessities dealt with, he climbed back into bed with me. "Come here, *angel moy*."

I let him tug me close to his soothing warmth and settled my cheek to his chest. "What does that mean?"

His fingertips moved up and down my cheek. "My angel."

I glanced up at him and smiled. "That's sweet."

Ivan tipped my chin and kissed me tenderly. "You are my little angel."

"Oh, I don't know about that." I drew my initials on his chest and traced the outline of a scar there. "I'm pretty sure what we just did was less than angelic."

He laughed, the rich baritone sound rolling through me. He started to reply but a loud snap echoed in the house. Everything running on electricity stopped working. Ivan stiffened and carefully shifted me out of his arms. I sat up and let my eyes adjust to the faintest sliver of moonlight streaming through the window where Ivan had gone.

"Maybe it's a blackout," I suggested. "You know how hard the grids get hit in the summer. Everyone runs their air conditioners at full blast."

"It's not a blackout." Ivan's tight voice scared me. "Get your shirt on and get in the closet."

"Wh-what?"

"Now, Erin!" He lowered his voice to a hiss. I didn't dare refuse his order. I scrambled to find my discarded shirt on the floor. Ivan found his way back to me and hopped into his pants. Before I could ask, he explained, "My neighbors have power. We're the only dark house. Someone's here."

"For me?" The awful reality struck me. "Oh god."

"No." Ivan grasped my shoulders. "You will not panic. Grab your phone. Get in the closet. Call 9-1-1."

"Okay." I snatched up my phone and let him push me into the closet. My hands trembled as I started to dial for help.

The glow from my phone lit up his face. "After you've made that phone call, you stay quiet. Not one noise from this closet, do you understand? Whatever you hear, you stay quiet and hide until the police arrive."

"Yes, Ivan."

He kissed me, his lips lingering for a second, before he stepped out of the closet and shut the door. I heard the low scrape of furniture moving and realized he was putting something heavy in front of the door. It dawned on me that maybe Kostya hadn't stayed like last night. Terrified by the thought of him alone out there, I hit dial and brought the phone to my ear.

As I waited for someone to answer, I tried to slow my frantic breathing. After the nightmare of the last 48 hours, I would have thought that I'd grown immune to such fear but apparently not. I squeezed myself into a tiny ball in the far corner of the closet and brought my knees to my chest.

"9-1-1, what is your emergency?"

"Someone just broke into my boyfriend's house. They cut the power." I forced my voice to remain calm even though I was freaking the fuck out inside.

"What is your address, ma'am?"

I blanked for a second before finally remembering the street name and the numbers adoring the curb. I rattled them off and waited for the dispatcher's instructions. She promised me that help was on its way—but then a gunshot tore through the silence of the house.

"Someone is shooting!"

"I heard that, ma'am." The dispatcher's concern came through loud and clear. "Are you in a safe spot?"

IVAN

"Yes, I'm in a closet upstairs." My heart beat wildly in my chest. "Please, hurry! My boyfriend—"

"Ma'am, we'll have units on scene in just a minute or two."

A minute or two? Oh god! What if Ivan had been hit? What if he was bleeding and needed me?

Another gunshot ripped through the night. I clapped a hand over my mouth and scurried to the door. There was no way I could get it open but I pressed my ear to the wood and listened. The sounds of a scuffle met my ears. There were loud grunts and the sound of skin impacting skin. A loud crash and shattering glass made me gasp.

"Ma'am? Are you all right? Is something else happening?"

"They're fighting." I whispered into my phone. "Please, you have to hurry."

"We are. Stay as quiet as possible."

She continued to talk but I tuned her out. I focused only on the sound of fighting in the bedroom. The brutal noises made my stomach lurch. If Ivan was fighting hand-to-hand, I had no doubt that he could hold his own but I'd heard gunshots. If there were weapons involved or if he was already hurt...

Something heavy hit the floor. Heavy boots slammed against the wooden planks. Someone was kicking, I realized. There was so much grunting and gasping—and then it became eerily quiet.

I held my breath and waited. Footsteps sent me rushing back from the door. I hugged the back wall of the closet and prayed it wasn't one of the monsters who had broken into the house. The furniture shoved in front of the door made an awful scratching sound as it slid across the floor. A moment later the door opened and I squeaked in fear.

But it was Ivan's hulking form that stood silhouetted in the doorway. I let loose an anguished, relieved cry as he knelt down in front of me. My phone hit the floor and I flung myself into his waiting arms. The slick sweat from his skin made him hard to grasp but I held on tight.

Our lips met in a seeking kiss. The metallic tinge of blood didn't bother me. I hated that he'd been hurt defending me but he was alive in my arms. That was all that mattered to me right now.

"Sh," he cooed and squeezed me tighter. "I've got you, Erin."

And I hoped he never let go.

6 CHAPTER SIX

Ivan hated police stations. They set his teeth on edge and brought back memories he'd just as soon forget. Of course, he hadn't ever been on this side of the equation. The experience of being taken in to give a report and interview was much different than being hauled out of bed and cuffed for committing some crime.

They kept the interview rooms unnecessarily cold. He noticed the way Erin shivered next to him. She wore jeans and a t-shirt with his jacket draped around her shoulders. He deduced it wasn't the chill that left her hands trembling but the post-adrenaline shakes from surviving such a brazen attack on their lives.

Wanting to reassure her, Ivan reached for her hand beneath the table and dragged it onto his leg. He glanced at her and winked. She smiled, just for him, and let some of the fear ease from her pretty face.

His face, on the other hand, didn't look so good. Taking down two armed men in the dark wasn't as easy as the movie stars made it look. He'd escaped the ordeal with only a black eye, busted mouth and gashes on his shoulders and arms. The two gunshots he'd narrowly missed had been pure luck.

It had been a long time since he'd felt real fear. The idea that those thugs had come into his home to hurt Erin had enraged him. Feeling bullets snap by his ear and slam into the wall behind him had turned that rage into fear. Not for himself but for Erin. He'd never forgive himself if anything had happened to her. The need to protect and defend her had spurred him onward, right into the face of danger.

"Well, Mr. Markovic, since you managed to de-escalate the situation without killing the two intruders, you saved yourself a hell of a lot of hassle." The detective from the gang unit finished scribbling his signature across the statements he and Erin had given. "Unfortunately, this won't be the last you see of me.

You'll both likely be called to testify if this goes to jury trial."

Ivan inwardly grimaced. The last thing he wanted was to be called to testify. He hoped those two idiots he'd put in headlocks and choked into submission would be smart enough to take a plea deal and spare everyone the headache.

There was a knock on the door to the interview room. A second later, a patrol officer poked his head into the room. "Sorry to interrupt but you're needed out here, Detective Santos."

"Sure." The detective smiled at them. "I'll be right back."

Ivan nodded and watched the man disappear. His inner alarm clanged. Was this some kind of game? It wasn't the first time two police officers had tried to pull this kind of ruse on him. He eyed Erin carefully and hoped she'd get the message he was trying to send. If those two men were listening in from the connected observation room, he didn't want Erin to accidentally say anything that might cause them more problems.

"Ivan?"

"Yes?" He reached out and touched her cheek.

"I'm sorry about all of this."

He shook his head. "Don't be. It's not your fault."

"Isn't it?"

"No, *angel moy*. It's—"

The door opened and the detective returned. He didn't come all the way into the room. Instead he said, "Miss Hanson, is your sister's name Ruby?"

Ivan's gut clenched. He silently prayed this detective wasn't about to tell them Ruby was dead.

Erin went rigid. "Yes."

"So I suppose I don't have to ask why those two Hermanos cockroaches were trying to kill the two of you," the detective said with a frown. He sighed and waved his hand. "You two should come with me. Your sister was picked up an hour ago. She's been in a cell downstairs but they brought her up here for questioning."

Ivan gripped Erin's hand as they left the interview room and trailed the detective to another room. They were led into a smaller, dimly lit space with a two-way mirror. Ivan let go of Erin's hand so she could make her way to the glass. She put her hand on it and stared at her sister.

Ivan had thought Ruby looked terrible last night when they'd found her in a pool of her own piss and vomit but she stunned him by looking even worse now. Her dirty hair hung in greasy clumps around her face. She'd found a pair of slacks and a blouse that looked like they belonged on a grandmother. Hell, they probably had! Knowing Ruby, she'd likely stolen them from another patient before escaping the hospital.

The sleeves of the white blouse were torn and blood-stained. Her hands had been bandaged. She had some small scrapes on her face and kept rubbing at her neck and forehead. In short, Ruby was in a bad, bad way.

"She was picked up breaking into a pharmacy not far from the hospital. She managed to sneak out of the hospital without any of the nurses or doctors seeing her." The detective hesitated. "One of our patrol officers reported warning her away from a known prostitution area around eight this evening. It looks like she tried to make some cash the old-fashioned way, and when that didn't work, she just broke into a pharmacy to get what she wanted."

Ivan hated that Erin had to hear all this. He cleared his throat. "I'll call a lawyer for her."

"She's going to need one." Detective Santos took a few steps toward Erin. "You know that she's being hunted by the Hermanos and the Albanians, right? I mean, if my informants have kicked that piece of information up to me here in the gang squad, you must know."

Erin nodded. "I do."

The detective glanced back at Ivan. "I know enough about your boyfriend to be damn sure that he knows exactly what kind of trouble the Albanians and Hermanos can make for you."

Ivan didn't even try to deny his history. It wasn't exactly a secret, after all. His interest remained on Erin. Her shoulders slumped with defeat. He desperately wanted to pull her into his arms and kiss away her fears but right now she had choices to make about her future.

"We found a body in a junk yard earlier this afternoon. It's Andrei Kominsky." Detective Santos dropped that bombshell without warning. "I'd heard that he was trying to muscle in on some Hermanos territory and had been stealing from the Albanians. I guess your sister is the girlfriend everyone on the street wanted to find."

Erin nodded. "Yes."

"It looks like the Albanians were the ones who finished him off. I'm just guessing here but I think they took out Andrei and left your sister's score to be settled by the Hermanos." Her met Ivan's stare. "After what happened in your home, I doubt you'll have to worry about those jerks coming back for more from the two of you. They'll respect your strong response."

"But Ruby?" Erin asked softly.

"If you bail her out, they'll come for her—and you might get caught in the crossfire."

IVAN

It was the ugly truth that Ivan had been hoping to spare Erin. What the detective wasn't saying was that it would be equally as difficult for the jail to keep Ruby safe from retribution on the inside.

"Look, she's a drug addict in need of rehab. When we're done questioning her, she's going to go straight to the special medical unit for addicts undergoing withdrawal. She'll be safe there for a few days. Maybe this thing with the Hermanos will have blown over by then."

Detective Santos shot Ivan a look that was easily interpreted. What he meant was that maybe Ivan would be able to use his contacts to iron out some kind of peace.

"And then what?" Erin asked, her voice wobbling with sadness.

"A good lawyer will get her into one of the rehab programs run by the jail. If she stays clean, she could do six months, maybe a year, and then probation."

"If she stays clean," Erin repeated skeptically.

Ivan couldn't blame her skepticism. When they'd been at the hospital, she'd told him all about the many times she'd taken Ruby to meetings and even arranged rehab. None of it had worked. Hopefully this nightmare experience would be the thing that helped Ruby get a grip on her life.

When Erin turned to face him, he saw the uncertainty etched on her face. "Ivan, what do I do?"

Even though it killed him to offer, he said, "I'll pay her bail, if you want to get her out tonight."

"Thank you." Erin inhaled slowly. "But no. I think I'm done bailing her out of trouble. She's never going to get better if I keep helping her escape the consequences."

Ivan knew how hard it was for Erin to do something so harsh but he respected her all the more for it. On the verge of tears, she hugged herself tightly. "May I see her?"

Detective Santos nodded. "I can give you a few minutes."

Ivan held out his hand and Erin came to him. He wrapped his arms around her small frame and hugged her tight. He brushed lips against her temple. "Go talk to Ruby. Make peace with her." He caressed her face. "I'll call a lawyer."

With a nod, Erin slipped out of his arms and followed the detective out of the room. Ivan took his phone from his pocket and scrolled through his list of contacts. The lawyer who handled the gym's business affairs answered on the fourth ring. "Jack, sorry to bother you so late at night but I need a favor..."

IVAN

My stomach ached as I entered the interview room where Ruby sat. Her panicked gaze found me. She started to weep into her bandaged hands. "Erin, I'm so sorry."

"Hey," I whispered and rushed to her. I crouched down and slipped my arms around her shaking shoulders. My nose wrinkled as the scents of dirt, blood and sweat hit my nose. "It's okay."

"It's not," she sobbed. "Andrei is dead. They killed him!"

"I'm so sorry, Ruby." Even though I hadn't liked her boyfriend, I'd never wanted him dead. Her painful sobs tore at me. Her whole world was crumbling around her and all I could do was offer a hug and my love.

"The police told me that some of the Hermanos tried to kill you." She sobbed even harder now. "I never meant for you to get hurt."

"I know you didn't." I rubbed her back. "I know you didn't mean for any of this to happen."

"But it did," she wailed.

I held her as she cried and tried to soothe her. "Ivan is hiring a lawyer right now. He's going to try to get you into the jail rehab program. The detective told me they'll keep you segregated from the other inmates to keep you safe."

She leaned back and searched my face. "You're not bailing me out?"

My chest constricted and I prepared for the inevitable screaming match. "No."

Her lower lip trembled. "Is it because I yelled at you in the hospital?"

"No, Ruby. That's not why." I pushed some of the dirty strands of hair behind her ear. "If I bail you out, you're going to run away from me and get high. I know it. You know it. You almost died last night. I can't—I won't watch you do it again."

She grew quiet and still. "Why do you still love me so much?"

I reeled backwards at her unexpected question. "What? Why would you ask me that?"

"I killed Mom and Dad."

"You did not!" I started to cry now. "It was just an accident, Ruby. Even if you had gotten home on time, you might not have realized the house was filling with carbon monoxide. You might have been killed—and then I would have been all alone." I squeezed her hands. "I need you, Ruby. We need each other."

Ruby cried, the tears streaming down her face and leaving clean lines on her dirt-smudged cheeks. "I want to get clean but I'm so scared."

"I know you are but you won't be doing it alone. There will be people to help you and I'll visit whenever I can. Even if I can't see you or talk to you, I'll be supporting you, Ruby. You're my sister and I love you." I cupped her cheek. "I love you, Ruby."

"I love you, Erin." She touched her forehead to mine. "I'm going to get clean. I swear it."

"I believe you." This time felt different than the others. I had no doubts that she was finally going to take control and face her demons.

She touched a spot on her arm and drew my attention. Her finger circled the strange drawing on her skin. It looked like a bird. Our gazes met and I frowned. I wanted to ask her what she was trying to tell me but she cut me off before I could even get a word out. "You need to go, Erin."

"I can stay a little longer."

She shook her head and wiped at her face. "No, I need you to go. If you stay, I'm going to lose my nerve and beg you bail me out. Go. Please."

"Okay." I gave her one final hug before rushing out of the interview room—and straight into Ivan's waiting arms. He didn't ask for the details and I was grateful. Instead, he took care of the last remaining items with the detective and ushered me out of the police station.

Outside, Dimitri and Kostya waited for us. No one spoke a word as we climbed into the SUV idling in the parking lot. Dimitri shot me a reassuring look from the front seat but it was Ivan's strong hand holding mine that kept me from having a complete breakdown during the ride back to his home.

At first, I couldn't believe that we were going back to his house, especially since it had no electricity and two men had just tried to kill us there. Finally, it occurred to me that going back there was Ivan's way of making a public statement. He wasn't going to be scared out of his home or allow anyone to strong-arm him.

Considering he'd just taken down a pair of armed assailants with nothing but his bare hands, I figured the Hermanos crew would get the message loud and clear. Ivan was not a man to be fucked with and he sure as hell wasn't going to let them touch me.

I was surprised to find Ivan's house teeming with men. Some of them I recognized from the gym. Others were strangers to me but obvious friends to Ivan. I didn't have to ask what they were doing there. It was clear they'd come to show support for Ivan.

IVAN

He stepped away from me just long enough to talk in quiet tones with Dimitri. His piece said, he took my arm and led me into the house. Someone had placed candles on the available flat surfaces. The subtle glow of candlelight lent a strange ambience to the place. Even so, a flashlight was thrust into Ivan's hand. He flicked it on and used it to light our way upstairs.

Instead of taking me to the guest room, he led me right into the master suite. He closed the door behind us and walked away from me just long enough to dig a long-handled lighter from a drawer. He lit some of the large scented candles on the dresser. The flickering flames glowed strangely on his shirt and skin.

Lowering the flashlight beam, he sank down into a big leather chair in the corner of his bedroom. "Come here, angel."

I ran to him, letting the jacket he'd given to me fall onto the floor. Sobbing, I hurled myself at him and snuggled up tight on his lap. Those powerful arms embraced me. I relished his heat and strength and found such comfort in his soft words and the hand stroking my hair.

"I know you're frightened but everything is going to be fine, Erin. I promise you. No one is going to harm you."

Guilt swamped me. I gingerly touched his bruised face. "I'm so sorry you got hurt, Ivan. When I came to you for help, I never imagined it would get this bad."

He took my hand and kissed my fingertips. "I gave you my protection knowing full well that it could escalate to this level." He held my gaze in the candlelight. "I'd do it all over again in a heartbeat."

He didn't need to say anything else. I understood then that his feelings for me were just as intense as mine were toward him. "I'm so glad I found you."

Smiling, he kissed me. "And I'm so glad you were brave enough to come into my gym. I can't imagine never meeting you."

"I know what you mean. I feel like my life has suddenly been separated into two halves—before Ivan and after Ivan."

He chuckled softly and nuzzled my neck. "It's the same for me."

The front of his shirt gaped open. I ran my finger over one of the onion dome tattoos visible there. In better light, the domes had a bluish tint and each one was capped by a small cross. "What do these mean, Ivan?"

He said something that sounded suspiciously like Russian cursing. "Angel, it's way too late to get into my sordid history. Let's leave it."

IVAN

I let my finger move along the tattoo. "But you will tell me eventually?"

"Yes." He kissed my forehead. "Someday soon, I'll tell you everything—and then you can decide."

"Decide what?"

"Whether you still want me."

He said it as though he feared I wouldn't. I wasn't naïve enough to think that his past was lily white. It was clear from the amount of ink I'd seen on his naked body that Ivan had lived a terrible life before getting onto a straighter path. I prayed that he hadn't done anything unforgivable.

As I traced his tattoo, my mind returned to the bizarre bird drawing Ruby had shown me. I was sure it meant something but what? I closed my eyes and tried to picture the symbol again. The blurry lines of blue ink became clear in my mind. What was she trying to tell me?

And then it hit me.

7 CHAPTER SEVEN

"It was a blue bird!" My head popped off Ivan's chest and I grinned at him. "A blue bird!"

He gawked at me as if I were a crazy person. "What are you—?"

"Ruby had a blue bird drawn on her skin. Bluebird Lane," I explained. "That's our house."

"Your house?" He frowned. "I thought you lived in an apartment."

"I do but we still own our old house. We lived in it until almost two years ago when we decided to put it on the market. The memories, you know?"

"But what does that have to do with Ruby?"

"If you needed to hide a shit load of drugs and money in a place where no one would look, wouldn't you choose a quiet house in an upper middle class neighborhood? We ended our realtor contract a few months ago. I got nervous that Ruby would spend all of her share on drugs so I convinced her that we should ride out the housing slump to get a better price. The place is just sitting there empty."

Ivan sat up straighter. "Where's your purse?"

"In the guest room."

"And your overnight bag that Vivi and Lena brought you at the hospital?"

"The same place. Why?"

"Let's go get them."

Not understanding why we needed my overnight bag, I nonetheless followed him into the guest room to grab it and my purse. Someone had cleared away all the busted up furniture and swept up the broken glass from the brutal fight that had taken place there. Still, the fine hairs on the back of my neck stood on edge as we entered the space.

In the hallway, we ran into Dimitri. Ivan spoke to him in Russian. For the first time since I'd met him, the fact that I couldn't understand what he was saying really annoyed me. I decided then and there that Vivi was going to have to tutor me in Russian as soon as possible.

As we followed Dimitri downstairs, I asked, "What are we doing?"

"You and I are going to get into my car and drive to a hotel."

"What? Why?"

"Because I'm certain we were followed by the police," he said, his voice so low I barely heard him. "They may think Ruby has told you where the drugs and money are hidden. It would be a huge win for them."

"Why don't we just tell them?" I wanted out of this gang war mess as quickly as possible.

Ivan frowned at me. In that moment, I realized how silly and naïve I must have seemed to him. "Erin, the Albanians have already killed Andrei to settle their blood debt but the Hermanos? They're still out there."

"So you want to trade whatever we find for Ruby's safety?"

"For your safety," he said and tugged me along beside him.

Within five minutes, I was buckled into the front seat of his black sports car. He raced away from his home in one direction while Dimitri went one way in his truck and Kostya took a different route in an SUV. The covert nature of Ivan's plane made my stomach ache.

"Are you all right?" He glanced over at me as he wound in and out of the late night traffic.

I rubbed my belly and grimaced. "I'm not used to this constant anxiety. I think I'm getting an ulcer."

"I doubt it, *angel moy*." He squeezed my thigh. "You've shown such bravery. I'm impressed."

Considering the kind of life he'd lived, I figured that was quite a compliment. "Thanks, I guess."

Ivan laughed and turned into a parking garage behind one of the upscale boutique hotels downtown. I thought it an odd destination until he addressed the guy running the private parking garage. Their quick conversation in Ivan's mother tongue and the mention of Dimitri's name helped me understand. This was just part of the ruse.

He reached into the console between our seats where he'd dropped his wallet before we left the house. My eyes widened when he withdrew a handful of crisp hundred dollar bills and thrust them into the parking attendant's hand. The man handed him a time-stamped ticket and hit the button to raise the black-and-white striped bar.

As Ivan drove up the many levels of the garage, it occurred to me that he still hadn't told me how he'd made all his money. "Is your money blood money?"

He visibly stiffened. I chewed my lower lip as nervousness swept through me. He found an empty spot on the fourth level and parked. After killing the engine, he let his hands drop from the wheel. He turned to face me. His expression was one I couldn't place.

"You must think the worst of me."

I gulped. "I don't really know what I think, Ivan. You have all those tattoos and you're obviously very comfortable in the underworld. Yesterday when I tried to ask you about your wealth, you shot me down."

"Time shares."

I blinked. "What?"

"Time shares," he repeated. "I made the bulk of my wealth in time shares."

I tried to wrap my head around what he'd said. "But—"

"Look, I'm no choir boy, Erin. I've done some terrible things. I've stolen. I've burglarized. I've enforced for loan sharks. I've moved drug shipments and run weapons. There was a time when I would do anything if the price was right."

The shame filling his voice touched me in a way I couldn't quite explain. I reached for his hand. "I'm sorry. I shouldn't have asked."

"No." He kissed my knuckles. "You have every right to know what kind of person I am."

"I think the man I know is a good man. God, what you've done for me, Ivan."

"It wasn't without ulterior motives," he replied honestly. "From the moment I saw you, I wanted you. Saving your sister was the easiest way for me to keep you near." He held my gaze. "I swear to you that I have never once committed any sort of crime against women. I've never dealt in the skin trade. I've never killed anyone. I'm no murderer and no rapist but I was a thief and a violent man."

"You've been in prison." It wasn't a question. Some of the tattoos he had looked like prison work with their uneven lines and strange blue tint.

"Three times," he admitted. His shamed gaze dropped to his lap. "I did my time, Erin. I paid for my crimes."

"And then what? You came to Houston and started over?"

He nodded. "Nikolai was leaving. The three of us— me, Nikolai and Dimitri—we had money. It cost so much to buy a new life but we managed it." He hesitated. "I won't sit here and lie to you about the way my life started in Houston. I dealt in stolen goods and bare-knuckle fighting to make enough money to invest."

"In time shares?" I couldn't hide my surprise. "I mean, *really?*"

His lips twitched with amusement. "I know. It's really just a legal scam, isn't it? But the money was so easy. Dimitri and I both bought into them when they were cheap and made money hand over fist. We listened to Yuri and got out before the real estate market went bust. I parked quite a bit of my money in minerals and oil and gas with Yuri's company. The returns have been...well...they've been substantial."

"And that's how you paid for your gym and started your training business?"

"Yes." He ran his thumb over the underside of my wrist. "I know it doesn't make it right but I donate to charities. Food banks and women's shelters and the children's hospital here. I send money back to Russia, to the orphanage there. It helps me feel like I'm paying for my sins."

"Oh, Ivan." I unbuckled my seatbelt and slid closer, winding my arms around his neck and hugging him tightly. "You made mistakes. We all do. Yours were pretty big ones but you've been punished for them. You're trying to make it right. I respect that."

He pulled back and gazed into my eyes. "And me? Can you respect me?"

"I do."

He buried his face in the curve of my neck. "I don't deserve you."

I kissed his cheek. "Don't say that."

"It's the truth," he insisted. "You're the type of woman who deserves a man with an education and a

clean criminal record. Someone you can be proud of—
and that's not me."

"That's not true." I cupped his face and kissed him
tenderly. "You saved my life. You saved my sister.
You fought to defend me from two men with guns.
You could have died, Ivan, but you faced them with-
out any thought for your own safety. Don't you see?
That's the kind of man you are."

His pale eyes widened briefly. "God, Erin," he said,
his voice thick with emotion. "You make me want—"

But he didn't get to finish his thought. Dimitri
chose that moment to knock on the driver's side window. I gritted my teeth with frustration. I'd been sure
that Ivan was about to say something amazing but
Dimitri had blundered right into the middle of it.

Ivan exhaled roughly and frowned. "We'll pick this
discussion up later. Yes?"

"Yes."

"Good." His lips lingered against mine. "Come. Let's
do this."

Ivan controlled the desire to throttle Dimitri for his poor timing. He'd never felt closer to Erin than when she'd been half across his lap while he poured out his darkest secrets. Her acceptance of his past had stunned him. She'd taken a reasonable stance on the crimes he'd committed and the punishment he'd served and seemed willing to accept that he was a different man today than the awful person he'd been when he'd done those things.

He would never stop trying to fix those wrongs. The charities he supported weren't enough—nothing could ever really clean away the smudges on his character—but they gave him a sense of peace. Knowing that Erin was willing to walk beside him without embarrassment or shame and with her head held high filled him with such strong hope. Maybe the life he'd always wanted wasn't so far out of reach after all.

"Do you see the entrance up ahead? Turn in there and then take the first right."

Ivan's gaze moved to the windshield. Erin gave Kostya instructions as they neared her childhood home. Dimitri followed in his truck not far behind.

The neighborhood she'd been raised in was filled with big houses and large yards. It was the kind of place he'd dreamed about as a hungry child living hand-to-mouth in an orphanage. Even though he'd surpassed his wildest dreams, he still had mornings where he woke in a daze, unable to believe he'd risen to such heights.

"The brick two story with the dark shutters," she said and pointed to a house near the cul-de-sac. While Kostya pulled into the driveway, she dug around in her purse and produced a key ring. He noticed the way she gripped the keys so tightly. Whether it was the painful memories of losing her parents in this house or the uncertainty of what they would find inside that left her so upset, Ivan couldn't say.

Out on the sidewalk, he gripped her hand. She started to take the lead but he stopped her. He held out his hand. "Give me the key."

"Why?" Erin asked but did as instructed.

"Because Andrei might have been stupid enough to booby trap the place," he said matter-of-factly. "You stay back with Dimitri and Kostya."

"No," Dimitri interjected. "I'll go first."

Ivan nodded and handed over the key. Those years in the military and later in Spetsnaz had given Dimitri quite a few skills Ivan would never possess.

He pushed Erin behind him and waited near the SUV while Dimitri unlocked and entered the house. A few minutes later, Dimitri returned. He shook his head and said, "You aren't going to believe what's in there."

Ivan's stomach clenched. "The drugs?"

"And the money and piles of stolen electronics," Dimitri added. "It's all there plus more."

"I can't believe she used our parents' house like this," Erin whispered, her voice laced with pain. "Doesn't she realize it can be seized?"

"I don't think she cared," Ivan replied bluntly. "But you bring up a good point. I don't want you to be any part of this."

"But—"

"No." He spoke firmly but gently took her hand to lead her a few feet away. Frustration radiated from her in waves. Running his fingers down her cheek, he said, "This is tricky business, Erin. I need to concentrate. I can't do that if I'm worrying about you."

"Oh." Her annoyance with him fled. "I didn't think of it that way."

"I want you to go back to the hotel and get a room there." He withdrew his wallet and discreetly slipped her a large sum of money. She started to argue with him but he silenced her with a demanding kiss. He plundered her mouth, stabbing his tongue between her lips, and tasting her until she whimpered in his arms.

She sighed softly and pressed her cheek to his chest. "Is that the way it's going to be? Every time I want to argue about something, you're just going to kiss me until I'm dizzy?"

He laughed. "It sounds like a good plan."

She rose on tiptoes and brushed her mouth against his. "A very good plan." Then, more seriously, she begged, "Please be careful, Ivan."

"I will. Text me the hotel room number. I'll be sliding into bed with you in no time."

"Promise?"

He kissed her forehead. "Promise."

Reluctantly, she made her way back to Kostya. He shared a look with his longtime employee. Kostya would protect Erin with the same vigor he had, if the need arose. Standing next to Dimitri, he watched the SUV until the tail lights disappeared from view.

Ivan turned to Dimitri. "Do you have a way to contact Besian?"

"Yes."

"And the Hermanos?"

He hesitated before nodding. "I can use Johnny to get a message through."

"Then do it and let's finish this."

8 CHAPTER EIGHT

Five Weeks Later

"We're having breakfast here?" Lena wrinkled her nose. "I'd hoped we were going someplace with mimosas on the menu."

I shot her a knowing look. She looked rumpled and worse for the wear this morning. "I think maybe you had enough to drink last night."

"I wish I'd had time to kick back a few shots last night," she grumbled. "This is exhaustion."

"You're a PR girl for one of the hottest clubs in Houston," Vivi replied. "How hard can that be?"

Lena shot her the finger. "That hard."

I snorted with amusement and shoved open the door to the bakery/café I'd come to love. "Dimitri introduced me to this place. The breakfast tacos and pastries here are to die for!"

"I'm not so sure about all these carbs," Lena said as she tucked her sunglasses into her oversized and ridiculously expensive purse. "I had to suck it in just to get into these jeans this morning."

"Then maybe you should try buying jeans in your actual size," Vivi suggested. "No one else sees the number but you, Lena."

She smacked Vivian's tiny butt and made her yelp. "When you finally get out of the toddler section, you can tell me all about buying jeans to fit a donkey booty."

I laughed but gave the pair a hand gesture to tell them to tone it down. The patrons of Benny's bakery weren't the type of crowd who would enjoy talk of big butts and skinny jeans.

As Vivian and Lena talked in hushed tones behind me, I glanced around the bakery. The Saturday morning breakfast rush seemed like good business. Most of the tables were full and the line to order was a decent size. Still, I knew from the little bit I'd pried from Dimitri that the place was struggling.

I caught sight of Benny coming out of the kitchen area. She balanced a huge tray of pastries one hand. Back behind the counter, she handed them off to one of her employees and moved down the line. She noticed me and smiled. Her bright grin infected me with happiness. I don't know that I'd ever met anyone as spunky or fun as Benny.

Before I could turn to tell Lena and Vivi about her, Lena made a strange sound. "Benny Burkhart?"

Laughing, Benny hurried out from behind the counter to hug Lena. "Oh my gosh! How long has it been?"

"Sophomore year at college," Lena said and hugged her back. "I heard you'd left school to help out with the family business. I had no idea it was a bakery!"

"This is it." Benny motioned around the cozy place. "I'm going to school part-time now. I need two semesters before I graduate."

"Good for you!" Lena shot me an annoyed look. "Why didn't you tell me Benny owned this place?"

"I didn't know you two were acquainted."

"We were in the same dorm freshman year," Benny explained. "We had a pretty good time together."

"Hell yes we did!" Lena's skilled eye jumped around the bakery. "Looks like you could use some marketing and PR help, Benny. This is a good location but you're not doing nearly as much business as you could."

Benny swallowed a bit nervously. "Those kinds of skills are expensive to hire."

Lena smiled warmly. "I'm sure we can work something out."

Benn looked surprised. "You're in PR now?"

Lena nodded. "I work at Hillman & Crest where I do mainly night clubs and restaurants but I know I can handle this. Why don't we trade contact info..."

When the line moved, Vivi and I left the two old friends behind to talk business. We placed our order and found a table. A short time later, Lena joined us with her coffee and breakfast burrito. She seemed rather excited about working with Benny.

"Isn't this a step down from the usual posh places you promo whore for?" Vivian asked.

Lena didn't deny it. "I won't do it on company time, obviously, but she's a really nice girl. It's clear she could use some help." She dumped a few tablespoons of sugar into her coffee and gave it a stir. Her gaze held mine. "So—how was it at the jail yesterday?"

I licked some of the sweet cinnamon filling that had oozed out of my pastry from my finger. With a grimace, I said, "It was okay. Jails are creepy places."

"Is Ruby doing well in treatment?" Vivi sipped her tea. "She's five weeks into it. That's better than she's ever done, right?"

I nodded. "She was...difficult during our visit. I could tell that she's depressed and having a hard time facing the consequences of what she's done. Being high as a kite for years made it easy to mask all the wrong she was doing. Now it's staring her right in the face. She's trying, though, and that's all that really matters."

Lena emptied a couple of creamer packets into her cup. "Has her lawyer finished hammering out her plea deal?"

"She's going to finish the six months of mandatory in-jail rehab and do another six months in an extended treatment program at the jail. Twelve months total," I said. "Then probation."

"Wow," Vivi said softly. "That's harsh but I guess she's just lucky to be alive."

"Absolutely," I agreed.

"Have you," Lena lowered her voice, "have you had any more problems with *you-know-who*?"

She meant the Albanians and the Hermanos. "No, they've left us all alone."

"Do you blame them?" Vivi asked. "Ivan put one of those guys in a halo brace and the other one had to have his leg rebuilt. I'm sure they're going to avoid you two like the plague."

"Speaking of Ivan," Lena said with a lascivious smile, "how are things with your big Russian hunk?"

My cheeks grew hot. "Very good."

"Oh come on!" She practically begged. "Details? *Please*! I live with a nun," she gestured to Vivi, "and I'm stranded in a sex desert where there isn't one good penis to be found."

Now my ears were bright red. I glanced around the tables surrounding us and prayed no one was eavesdropping. "Not here! Maybe later."

"No maybe to it, Erin. I'm going to get all the juicy, dirty details from you."

Vivi rolled her eyes and whacked Lena's arm. "Calm down! You're worse than a frat boy."

Lena looked contrite. "Yes, Sister Vivian."

I laughed as the two roommates and longtime friends pinched and smacked one another. When they were done with their childish play, they laughed and turned back to me. Both stared expectantly and I realized they wanted to hear more about my relationship with Ivan. I figured now was as good a time as any to tell them.

"So—Ivan wants me to go back to school in the fall and work on my MBA. I was hoping to turn my part-time gig at the firm into full-time employment but they've made it clear they're going to downsize. I won't be kept on as an accountant. I was toying with the idea of going to grad school but it's so expensive. Ivan offered to help." I hesitated. "And he wants me move in with him."

Instead of the cries of outrage at the idea of moving in so quickly with him, they both looked rather calm. Finally, Vivi spoke. "Well—are you going to?"

"What? Go back for my MBA or move in with him?"

"Both," she clarified.

I chewed my lower lip and admitted, "I'm leaning toward yes on both."

"But?" Lena asked.

"But it's a big step, right? Moving in with him and letting him help me with school?"

"Dude!" Lena gaped at me as if I were dumb. "The man saved your sister from two bloodthirsty gangs and fought off two armed dickheads with his bare hands! How the heck do you say no to that?"

"She's right," Vivi agreed. "Look, I'm always the one who says be careful and stay away from guys like Ivan but not this time. I know he's not perfect and he's done some shady things in his past but he's reformed himself. He's a standup guy—and he loves you."

I couldn't deny that. He hadn't said it outright but I wasn't blind. Ivan loved me just as much as I loved him.

I put my head in my hands. "Maybe I'm just scared that moving in with him is going to ruin it. What we have is so special. I don't want to lose that."

"You won't." Lena spoke with authority. "I'm not the sappy, lovey-dovey, fate type, you know? But when I look at you two? It makes me hope that some-day I'll have someone like Ivan in my life." She paused. "Just without the criminal record."

I threw a piece of pastry at her, whacking her right in the face. "Bitch!"

She laughed and brushed the pastry onto the table. "I've got enough male criminals in my life. I don't need one sharing my bed."

Lena said it with a smile but I could hear the pain in her voice. It couldn't have been easy to have a father who was known as the best fence in Houston or a cousin who was in and out of juvie and now working as her dad's protégé.

"Sorry, Lena."

She waved it off. "We can't pick our family."

I smiled at Vivi and Lena. "No but I think we did a good job picking our friends."

Later that afternoon, I puttered around the apartment. I wandered by the door to Ruby's room and opened it. Nothing in her room had changed since I'd gone through and cleaned it last week. I hadn't had the heart to box up her things but if I decided to move in with Ivan it would have to be done. I wasn't at all sure how she was going to take that news. Badly, I presumed.

But I couldn't keep living my life worrying about Ruby. I'd been putting her and her problems first for so long that I'd been neglecting my life.

What I hadn't told Vivi and Lena was that my boss at the accounting firm had made it clear that he would have fought for me to be retained as a full-time employee if I'd been more reliable. I'd wanted to explain that cutting out of work early or coming in late had been caused by Ruby's craziness but I'd kept my lips zipped. He was right. I hadn't been reliable. I was the only to blame for that.

A knock at the door interrupted my troubled thoughts. I wasn't expecting anyone but it wasn't unusual to have the maintenance crew come by to change air conditioner filters during the summer. I lifted up on my bare toes to peek through the peep hole. My heart raced at the sight of Ivan's face and I couldn't get the door opened fast enough.

"Hey!"

"Angel." Ivan grinned and slipped off his sunglasses. He tucked them into the front pocket of his suit jacket. "I wanted to take you out to lunch but something came up so I decided I'd leave the gym a little early to spend the rest of the day with you."

I grasped his hand and tugged him inside the apartment. He kicked the door closed behind him and slid an arm around my waist. I let him drag me tight to his chest and surrendered to his searching kiss. He tasted of the cinnamon candies I'd learned he liked so much. His tongue swept mine before he nibbled my lower lip and reluctantly released me.

"How was breakfast with the girls?"

"Fun." I touched his hand. "You want some tea?"

"Yes, please." He shrugged out of his jacket and draped it over a chair before following me into the kitchen. I grabbed a glass from the cabinet and reached into the refrigerator for the pitcher of sweet tea I'd mixed that morning. He wasn't a huge fan of the cold stuff but after I'd nearly blown up the micro- wave trying to boil a mug of water to make him hot tea during our first week together, he'd graciously decided that iced tea was just fine.

When I turned around to offer him the glass, I found him sitting at my small dining table and thumbing through a Russian language workbook. Amusement glinted in his pale eyes. "What's this, angel moy?"

I slid the tea onto the table next to him. "Vivi gave it to me this morning. She's going to tutor me in Russian."

A look of utter adoration crossed his face. "For me?"

I trailed my fingers along his strong jaw. "You already speak my language. I think it's only fair that I learn to speak yours."

Ivan pulled me down onto his lap. His fingers sifted through my hair. "Should I work up a system of rewards for good scores on your tests?"

A thrill of excitement raced through my belly. "Depends on the reward."

His lips skimmed my throat. "Oh, I can think of a few things that would motivate your studies."

"Like?"

His hand slipped under my skirt and between my thighs. "How about this?"

I gasped as his fingertips slid inside my panties. He gently petted the seam of my sex. "Or maybe you'd prefer my tongue here?"

IVAN

I shuddered in his brawny arms. His skillful tongue had reduced me to tears of absolute joy last night. I'd never known orgasms could be that powerful. "You know I would."

He forced my thighs wide open and brushed his thumb across my clit. "Move in with me, Erin, and you can have this every morning and every night."

"I—"

Ivan kissed me, silencing my protest with his masterful mouth. "You belong with me, Erin. In my bed. In my home. In my arms. I love you, angel, and I know you love me."

"Yes," I whispered against his lips.

His hand went still between my thighs. "Yes you love me? Yes you belong with me? Or yes you will move in with me."

"All of it." I captured his mouth in a sensual kiss. "I love you. I belong to you."

"Always?"

I whimpered as his fingers began to torment me. Sitting there on his lap, I knew there was nothing I couldn't face with my big, sexy Russian protector in my corner. I brushed my lips across his and promised, "Always."

ROXIE RIVERA

IVAN

AN AUTHOR'S NOTE

I hope you enjoyed the first installment of the *Her Russian Protector* series! The series continues with full-length novels DIMITRI, YURI, NIKOLAI, SERGEI, SERGEI II and NIKOLAI II. Upcoming books in 2014 include new tales for Kostya, Alexei and Danila.

The series also inspired two spinoffs—The Fighting Connollys and Debt Collection series.

The Fighting Connollys focuses on brothers Kelly, Jack and Finn, three Marines fighting to save their family legacy and to protect the women they love. IN KELLY'S CORNER, IN JACK'S ARMS, and IN FINN'S HEART are available now in ebook and print.

IVAN

The Debt Collection series focuses on Besian Be-
ciraj's crew. It includes COLLATERAL (available now
in ebook and print) and the upcoming books COL-
LATERAL II, PAST DUE, PAID IN FULL, DOWN
PAYMENT and FINAL INSTALLMENT.

ABOUT THE AUTHOR

A *New York Times* and *USA Today* bestselling author, I like to write super sexy romances and scorching hot erotica. I live in Texas with a husband who could easily snag a job as an extra on History Channel's new *Viking* series and a sweet but rowdy preschool-aged daughter.

I also have another dirty-book writing alter ego, Lolita Lopez, who writes deliciously steamy tales for Ellora's Cave, Forever Yours/Grand Central, Mischief/Harper Collins UK, Siren Publishing and Cleis Press.

You can find me online at www.roxierivera.com.

Roxie's Backlist

Her Russian Protector

Ivan (Her Russian Protector #1)
Dimitri (Her Russian Protector #2)
Yuri (Her Russian Protector #3)
A Very Russian Christmas (Her Russian Protector #3.5)
Nikolai (Her Russian Protector #4)
Sergei (Her Russian Protector #5)
Sergei, Volume 2
Nikolai, Volume 2 (Her Russian Protector #6)—Coming June 2014

Kostya (Her Russian Protector #7)—Coming Summer 2014

Alexei (Her Russian Protector #8)—Coming Fall 2014

Danila (Her Russian Protector #9)—Coming Fall 2014

The Fighting Connollys

In Kelly's Corner (Fighting Connollys #1)
In Jack's Arms (Fighting Connollys #2)
In Finn's Heart (Fighting Connollys #3

Debt Collection

Collateral (Debt Collection #1)

Collateral II (Debt Collection #2)—Coming Soon

Past Due (Debt Collection #3)—Coming Soon

Paid in Full (Debt Collection #4)—Coming Soon

Down Payment (Debt Collection #5)—Coming Soon

IVAN

Final Installment (Debt Collection #6)—Coming Soon

Her SEAL Protector

Close Quarters

Seduced By...

Seduced by the Loan Shark
Seduced by the Loan Shark 2—Coming Soon!
Seduced by the Congressman
Seduced by the Congressman 2

Erotica

Chance's Bad, Bad Girl
Halftime With Craig
Tease
Eddie's Cuffs 1
Eddie's Cuffs 2
Eddie's Cuffs 3

ROXIE RIVERA

Disturbing the Peace
Quid Pro Quo
Search and Seizure

IVAN

Made in the USA
Middletown, DE
24 September 2021